His eyes speared hers as he straightened, too, rocking back on his heels. "You thought I knew about Jesse?"

"Yes, I did." Her eyes narrowed. "Are you suggesting that I am ashamed of my son?"

"I wouldn't dream of making such an accusation," he snapped.

"Then what's the big deal, Simon?"

But she knew what the big deal was. She and this man had forged a connection from the moment they'd swapped day-from-hell stories. The thought of her with another man infuriated him. Just like the thought of him with another woman curved her fingers into claws.

It made no sense. It couldn't go anywhere, but it existed.

He seized her wrist, brought his face close to hers and slugged her with a super-duper dose of his scent. She wanted to swoon.

"If I'd known you were a mother I would never—"

He broke off, released her wrist.

"What?" she challenged, glancing around to make sure their exchange hadn't given rise to any curious

d it of

ve kissed

Dear Reader,

What an exciting year—Harlequin is turning sixty! For sixty years Harlequin has provided uplifting, emotionally satisfying, life-affirming stories for its readers—stories that have reflected the changing attitudes of society, stories that have encouraged women to reach for their dreams.

When I was growing up, I was surrounded by women who read Harlequin romances—most of the women in my family, and many of the women who lived in the small country town where I lived. The shelves of the local library were filled with these wonderful books, which packed such an emotional punch. The stories thrilled, but more than that they helped instill a sense of optimism for life. I firmly believe that these books have made the world a happier place.

I'm honored that my stories have found such a wonderful home and I'm awed to be part of such a wonderful tradition. Happy anniversary, Harlequin.

Warmest wishes,

Michelle

MICHELLE DOUGLAS

The Aristocrat and the Single Mom

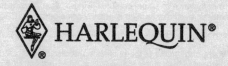

TORONTO • NEW YORK • LONDON
AMSTERDAM • PARIS • SYDNEY • HAMBURG
STOCKHOLM • ATHENS • TOKYO • MILAN • MADRID
PRAGUE • WARSAW • BUDAPEST • AUCKLAND

Recycling programs
for this product may
not exist in your area.

ISBN-13: 978-0-373-17576-5
ISBN-10:   0-373-17576-0

THE ARISTOCRAT AND THE SINGLE MOM

First North American Publication 2009.

Copyright © 2009 by Michelle Douglas.

At the age of eight, **Michelle Douglas** was
asked what she wanted to be when she grew up. She
answered, "A writer." Years later she read an article
about romance-writing and thought, Ooh, that'll be
fun. She was right. When she's not writing, she can
usually be found with her nose buried in a book. She is
currently enrolled in an English master's program for
the sole purpose of indulging her reading and writing
habits further. She lives in a leafy suburb of Newcastle,
on Australia's east coast, with her own romantic
hero—husband Greg, who is the inspiration behind all
her happy endings. Michelle would love you to visit
her at her Web site, www.michelledouglas.com.

Look out for Michelle Douglas's
next Harlequin Romance®
Bachelor Dad on Her Doorstep
coming in August 2009

To Bryony Green and Sally Williamson.
Your editorial input made all the difference.
Thank you.

CHAPTER ONE

KATE reached the last item in the file, closed her eyes, closed the file and counted to ten. Then she opened her eyes, opened the file and started again. The bell above the door jangled, telling her someone had entered the office, but she didn't move from her crouch in front of the filing cabinet. In fact, it was hard to move at all with all the boxes piled around her.

'Hello?'

At any other time a voice like that would've had her swinging around in curiosity…and anticipation. The voice was deep and masculine, with an intriguing British burr. A lot of tourists with a lot of different accents passed through this part of the world and Kate loved accents. She'd once meant to travel to some of those faraway places and immerse herself in different cultures, different languages. But that was before she'd fallen pregnant with Jesse. This particular accent, though, was her all-time favourite and could turn her insides to mush in the space of a heartbeat.

'I won't be a moment,' she called.

Half hidden by the desk, her customer probably couldn't see her. And although she usually made it a point to deal with prospective customers first, she took a deep breath and carefully examined the file again, lifting out and checking each document before moving to the next one.

Darn it. It wasn't there. Where had she put it? The accountant had wanted it last week. She'd promised to get it to him today. She slapped the side of the filing cabinet as if it were its fault. She glanced around at all the boxes and groaned.

'Is something wrong?'

She couldn't resist that accent any longer. 'I'm sorry.' She turned. 'I…'

She blinked. Air squeezed out of her lungs. Oh, dear Lord, who cared about finding receipts for boat repairs when a man like this stood in her office?

She tried to catch her breath, but it flitted in and out of her lungs with more speed than grace, evading her every attempt to harness it. She thought she ought to stand, but the longer she stared at him the more the world tilted to one side and, as she had no desire to fall flat on her face at his feet, she decided she'd better stay right where she was. Very carefully, she lowered her knees to the ground so she knelt rather than crouched. More stability—that was what she needed. And breakfast. She absolutely, positively shouldn't have skipped breakfast. Low blood sugar and all that.

She tried to hold back a sigh, but her mystery man had such a beautiful face to go with the beautiful British accent—not to mention a superb body—and it had been a long time since she'd beheld such a perfect example of masculine beauty that she had no hope of containing it. It came out on one long low breath. His too-short hair, as far as she could tell, was his single flaw. But it gleamed rich and dark in the half-light of her office and she could imagine its crispness against her palms with more clarity than sense.

She shook herself. 'Hello.' Her voice came out normal. She had no idea how. She even managed a smile.

'Hello,' he said again in that to-die-for accent, but he said it slowly, as if making a discovery. Then he smiled. Firm, sensual lips. Cheek creases.

The world abruptly stopped tilting and something slammed into her stomach with the impact of a missile. It felt wrong and right—both at the same time. It didn't make sense.

The man's eyes widened, his lips pursed for a brief moment, and she wondered if he'd felt the impact too.

Another sigh welled up inside her. And yearning. She expelled the sigh on one hard breath, but could do nothing with the yearning. She forced herself to her feet. 'I'm sorry to have kept you waiting.'

She glanced at the clock on the wall behind him—eleven a.m. The day was yet young. She had plenty of time to find receipts for boat repairs and visit her accountant. She had all the time in the world.

'Is everything all right?'

Just in time she stopped herself from saying, *It is now*, because that was crazy talk. Fanciful.

She was a single mother with a child. She didn't do fanciful. Not any more.

Her tourist had dark eyes that crinkled at the corners. They were nice eyes and they looked at her with concern. 'I'm sorry. Yes, I'm fine. Just a bit distracted.' By him. But she didn't want him to know that.

She blew a strand of hair out of her face and ordered herself to stop ogling the poor man, decided she'd buried herself in her work for far too long and that she'd better start getting out a bit more. 'I'm just having one of those mornings, you know?'

'Yep.' He gave one hard nod. 'Know exactly what you mean. Today, I can absolutely relate to that.'

Their gazes met and a surge of fellow feeling passed between them. In the dim light of her office she couldn't work out if his eyes were brown or dark grey. She'd need to be closer to tell for sure, but they were clear and direct and she found herself liking them.

Her day suddenly started to look up. 'How can I help you?' She pulled the reservation book towards her.

He smiled again and her knees gave a funny little wobble. She'd bet she looked a wreck. She resisted the urge to pat down her hair and straighten her shirt.

He didn't look a wreck. He looked impeccable in a charcoal-grey suit. Italian, she'd bet. Actually, she wouldn't know an Italian suit if it leapt up and bit her on the nose. It could be Bond Street for all she knew.

She knew shoes though, and those shoes were definitely Italian leather.

'I actually want to speak to your employer, Kate Petherbridge.'

Kate blinked.

'I was here at nine o'clock this morning.' He pointed to the glass door, which had the office hours printed across it. The previous owner's office hours. Kate hadn't got around to having them changed yet. 'Nobody showed up, which at the time I thought pretty unprofessional.'

She'd moved into this office two days ago. She'd figured they'd need the extra room at home now. But there was still so much to do. Her shoulders started to sag. He smiled again. Her knees gave another funny wobble. Outside, a magpie started to warble.

'But if you're having one of those kinds of days then—' he shrugged '—it can't be helped.'

He glanced down at the items spread across her desk—the contents of her bag drying out after their dunking in the bay. Without warning, the strap had given way when she'd raced the passenger list down to Archie. It was her best shoulder bag too. Only quick reflexes had saved the bag, contents and all, from sinking to the bottom to lie cradled against the oyster-encrusted rocks metres below. They seemed a paltry treasure—two bank cards, her driver's licence and medical card, a diary-cum-address book, the little paper money she'd had on her, a tab of aspirin that for some reason she hadn't thrown away, and a couple of soggy photographs. The one of Danny and Felice before they'd set off on their honeymoon was completely ruined.

'My bag fell in the bay.'

It was a completely ludicrous statement—self-evident—but the man opposite didn't laugh. He nodded as if he understood.

'That was right after I'd buried Moby—the goldfish.' That

had not been a good start to the day. It was why she'd taken her favourite shoulder bag—to try and cheer herself up.

'I'm sorry.'

'Thank you.'

He lifted one hand. 'For what it's worth, I hit a kangaroo in my hire car this morning.'

Even as she winced at the picture his words created, Kate decided then and there that their joint dispiriting tales of woe made this man a good omen. 'How fast were you travelling?'

'Eighty kilometres an hour.'

She winced again. Kangaroos didn't survive eighty-kilometre-per-hour collisions.

He suddenly shook himself. He leaned forward and offered his hand. 'I'm Simon Morton-Blake.'

Kate placed her hand inside his immediately. His long fingers curled around hers and he squeezed briefly. She squeezed back. They both smiled. His hair gleamed richer, darker. Reluctantly, or so it seemed to Kate, their hands parted company again. 'Pleased to meet you. I'm—'

The smile slid off her face. 'What did you say your name was?'

'Morton-Blake. Simon.'

What?

His eyes narrowed. 'Why? Do you recognise it?'

Of course she recognised it, but Felice hadn't mentioned anything about family.

'The full title is Simon Morton-Blake, the seventh Lord of Holm—' his lips twisted in self-derision '—but I don't expect you've heard of that.'

Her jaw dropped. 'You're a lord? Like…a real lord?'

'I am. Are you impressed?'

He raised an eyebrow and she wasn't sure who he was sending up—her or himself.

'It doesn't seem to hold much cachet in Australia,' he commented.

'No, I don't suppose it does, but…' she peered up at him

'...do you, like, have your own castle?' She could imagine him living in a castle. She could imagine him in a kilt.

Don't be ridiculous! He's English, not Scottish.

Still...she'd give a lot to see him in a kilt.

'The estate does have a fifteenth-century manor house and quite a few sheep, but no castle, I'm afraid. Not even the ruins of a castle.' He gave a mock grimace. 'Have I fallen in your estimation?'

Kate laughed. Even though his name was Morton-Blake and he had to be some kind of relative of Felice's. Even though Felice hadn't mentioned anything about family, let alone family as distinguished as the seventh Lord of Holm.

He must be a distant cousin or something. Perhaps Felice had sent him a postcard extolling the beauties of Port Stephens—and it had many—and how much fun she was having working for Kate's dolphin tour business.

But why hadn't she mentioned him? Why had Felice let Danny and Kate think she had no family at all?

'And you are?'

Kate snapped back to attention. 'Oh, I'm sorry.' She drew in a breath, tried to smile. 'I'm Kate Petherbridge.'

His face darkened and his eyebrows drew down low over his eyes as he placed his hands on her desk and leaned across it towards her. His eyes weren't brown but a dark smoky-grey.

'Then perhaps you can tell me where the hell my sister is?'

Very slowly, Kate sat. 'Sister?' Her mouth went dry. 'Felice is your sister?'

'Yes!' he shouted. 'And I want to know if she's okay.'

She sensed the concern behind his anger. 'Of course she is.' She made her voice crisp and businesslike, wanting to allay his worry as quickly as she could. 'Felice is perfectly fine and dandy.'

He closed his eyes, dragged a hand down his face and fell into the seat opposite. 'Thank God for that.'

His lovely broad shoulders went suddenly slack and it was only then that Kate realised how tightly he'd held himself. She frowned. She knew what it was like to worry about a younger sibling.

'I didn't know Felice had family.' In fact, Felice had led them to believe she was alone in the world. If Simon was a lord, what on earth did that make Felice?

And, more importantly, did Danny know?

Simon's eyes narrowed and his lips thinned. 'So that's the game she's playing, is it? Nevertheless, I am her brother. Are you doubting my verisimilitude?'

Kate wanted to close her eyes and wallow in that accent. She wanted to ask him to say that word again so she could watch the way his lips shaped it. She forced her spine to straighten instead. 'Do you have any proof?'

He leaned towards her again. 'You really don't believe me?'

She didn't know if he was angry or intrigued. 'I don't take risks with my staff's safety, Mr Morton-Blake.' Former staff's safety, she amended silently. Felice wasn't staff any more. She was family. 'I don't know you from Adam and I only have your word that you're who you say you are. For all I know, you could be stalking Felice.'

He sat back and folded his arms. 'And what if I am? What would you do?'

'I have a black belt in judo.' Which was the truth. 'And a spear gun in my desk drawer.' Which wasn't. 'I wouldn't try anything if I were you.'

Her desk drawer!

She clapped a hand to her head. Then she flung the drawer open. There it sat. Right on top—the file containing all the receipts her accountant had demanded from her—receipts that would save her from being fined by the Taxation Department. She didn't remember putting it there, but she pulled it out and kissed it all the same.

Simon had pulled back as if he expected her to draw a gun. Now his lips twitched at the corners, hinting at those cheek creases. 'My day just got a whole lot better,' she confided.

'I'm glad.'

He actually sounded as if he meant it. He pulled a wallet from his inside jacket pocket and flicked through it. It gave her a chance to study him. If he lived here in Port Stephens she'd bet the sun would bleach the tips of his hair. Simon Morton-Blake might be a lord but he didn't look as if he spent the majority of his time indoors behind a desk. If he lived around here she had a feeling he'd spend more of his time in the sun than out of it. Not that he was tanned, of course. England was only just emerging from winter. But he had a rugged outdoor aura that she recognised because she had it too.

And he had mentioned something about sheep.

He held a card out to her. 'My international driver's licence.'

His name—Simon Morton-Blake—stared back at her in official black and white type.

'And a photograph of me with my sister.'

Kate took it. Felice, Simon and another couple—older—all stared out from it with a formal reserve Kate found difficult to associate with Felice. She couldn't see anything of Felice in Simon's face, but she could see both Simon and Felice in the older couple—their parents?

'Our mother and father,' he said, as if she'd asked the question out loud. 'And no, they are no longer living.'

At least Felice hadn't lied about that.

She handed him back the licence and the photograph, wondering at how easily he could read her face. 'I'm sorry.'

He didn't say anything. He didn't glance back down at the photograph. He didn't even shrug.

With both parents dead... 'Do you have any other siblings?'

'No.'

That made Felice his only close relative. It went some way to explaining his concern.

'May I call you Simon?'

He smiled again. The grey of his eyes lightened. 'Please.'

Even though she was sitting, her knees still wobbled. 'Simon, why were you worried about Felice?'

'I haven't heard from her in over two months.' He raked a hand back over his hair. 'And her mobile isn't working.'

'It took a dunk in the bay,' Kate said carefully. 'Occupational hazard, I'm afraid.' She shrugged, trying to appear casual, but her mind raced. Why hadn't Felice contacted him? Why hadn't Felice told him about her marriage to Danny?

And what on earth was Kate supposed to do about it?

Not that Danny and Felice had told anyone about their marriage yet. They'd only told Kate because they'd wanted time off. She could understand them wanting to hug their secret close to their chests for a bit and enjoy a honeymoon idyll, but surely Felice could've found the time to let her only brother know?

'If…if you knew Felice was working for me, why didn't you give me a call or email me?' She could've allayed his worry and put his mind at rest in an instant.

He lifted his chin. His eyes glittered. 'I want to see Felice in the flesh. I want to see for myself that she's okay and not in any trouble.'

In trouble? Felice was twenty-two. Old enough to make her own decisions. Old enough to make her own mistakes. Old enough to look after herself.

'She's not in any kind of trouble.'

He ignored that. 'When can I see her?'

Kate's office suddenly shrank. Perhaps it was all that bristling over-protectiveness emanating from the seventh Lord of Holm that had the walls closing in on her, making him loom larger in her field of vision, making her notice the shape of his lean lips. Lips pressed tightly together, but it didn't stop her from imagining those lips on hers and…

Fresh air and food, that was what she needed, and the warmth of the sun on her shoulders. 'C'mon.' She rose and started for the door.

Simon followed her, watching closely as she locked the door

behind them. 'Are you going to take me to her?' he asked, staring at her as if he couldn't believe it would be that easy.

'I'm taking you for coffee.' Of course it wasn't that easy.

'I don't want coffee!'

Up this close, he smelt like wood shavings and cooler climes. She held her breath and reminded herself about the warmth of the sun—it'd help melt any ridiculous fantasies. 'But I do.'

He glared at her for a moment, then he visibly shook himself, his eyes cleared and he smiled. 'And you don't know me from Adam.'

She couldn't believe how quickly he could change from indignant prickliness to this…this melt a girl with his yumminess. She couldn't help but smile back. 'That's right.'

The problem was, she felt as if she *did* know him—a whole lot better than any Adam she'd ever met. Which was nonsense…and dangerous. It should frighten her off, but it didn't.

Kate's office was located in a small arcade. She led Simon down the tunnel of shop fronts to the bright February sunlight pouring in at one end, then turned right into Kelly's café.

'Flat white, cappuccino, latte…espresso?' she asked.

'Whatever.'

His voice drifted to her, slow and bemused. She glanced around and found him staring out at the view. She suppressed a grin. On a day like this, with the sun sparkling off the water in a thousand different points of light and the white hulls of the yachts at anchor in the marina gleaming, the sand golden and the sky blue, the bay looked spectacular. Couple it with the sounds of holidaymakers and the squawking of seagulls, the smell of salt and coconut oil, and most people were lost.

The seventh Lord of Holm was definitely lost.

'Would you like something to eat? A muffin?' Her stomach rumbled its approval. She hadn't had time for breakfast this morning, and Kelly's triple-choc muffins were to die for.

'No, thank you.' He didn't glance away from the view.

She wasn't eating if he wasn't. With her luck, she'd end up with chocolate muffin all over her face and that so wasn't the look she was after.

'Two flat whites, please,' she said to the waiting Kelly. 'In mugs.'

'Settling into your office, hon?'

'It's a mess.' She fished around in her pocket for change. 'I don't think I'll ever find anything ever again.'

'And when she does,' Simon said, snapping back around to the counter and holding out a twenty-dollar note to Kelly before Kate could free her hand from her pocket, 'she kisses it in gratitude.' He winked. 'That kind of behaviour can have a strange effect on a guy. She needs to be more careful.'

Kelly laughed. So did Kate—in complete and utter surprise. Not to mention delight. 'If I'd known the sun would have such a beneficial effect on your mood I'd have dragged you out here ten minutes ago.' But then she had visions of kissing Simon with a whole lot more fervour than she'd kissed her missing file of receipts and she started burning up from the inside out.

'Kelly,' she said hastily, 'this is Felice's brother, Simon.'

'Nice to meet any family of Felice's.' Kelly stared at him in open curiosity. 'Felice was the hit of the summer.' Then she winked at Kate. 'You going to put him to work on your boat?'

Kate cocked her head to one side and pretended to consider it. 'He's got arms that look like they could hold a boat steady.'

'He's got arms that look like they could hold a whole lot more than that, hon.'

Simon laughed.

Kate's imagination supplied her with more images than she knew what to do with. Heat blazed through her and she couldn't think of a single comeback.

Kelly took pity on her. 'Go and find yourselves a table. I'll bring the coffees out when they're ready.'

'Thanks, Kelly.'

Kate chose a table outside in the shade with a magnificent

view of the bay, but it didn't cool the heat circling through her. She tried to remember the last time she'd been on a date.

She had to remind herself that *this* wasn't a date.

Back to business. 'Are you and Felice close?'

His smile disappeared. 'Of course we are.'

Kate noticed his telling hesitation, the pause before the rough 'Of course'.

His spine stiffened. 'We're family.'

She took in the expression on his face. Her chest expanded and her back tightened. 'Want to tell me about it?'

His face closed up. 'There's nothing to tell.'

She tried a different tack. 'No offence, but I know for a fact that Felice is twenty-two. You don't exactly look…' She trailed off with what she hoped was delicate tact.

A glimmer of a smile appeared in the grey eyes. 'I'm ten years older than Felice.'

Kelly set their coffees in front of them. 'Thank you,' Kate murmured, and although she sensed Simon was immersed in thoughts of Felice, he still roused himself to send Kelly a smile of thanks that put a spring in the other woman's step.

It was a nice thing to do.

She had a feeling that, beneath all his bristling worry and concern, Simon Morton-Blake was a nice man.

'Ten years is a pretty big age gap between siblings,' she observed.

'It is,' he agreed.

He took a sip of his coffee. Frown lines marred the perfection of his face. He took a second sip and Kate wondered if he even tasted it. Kelly did the best coffee on the bay, but it looked as if great coffee was wasted on the seventh Lord of Holm today.

'Felice has always been too reckless and irresponsible.' He glanced up and speared her with his clear grey gaze. 'What did Kelly mean when she said Felice was the hit of the summer?'

'That she was popular, fun. That everyone liked her.'

His mouth grew grim. 'That's what I was afraid of.'

She wanted to ask why, but she bit her tongue. Beneath the table she selected Felice's number on her mobile, then brought the phone to her ear. Simon's eyes narrowed in on the phone in the space of a heartbeat. 'She was neither reckless nor irresponsible working for me.' Kate crossed her legs and waited for Felice to answer. 'In fact, she was a great worker.'

He nearly dropped his coffee. 'Felice?'

'Hey, it's me,' Kate said when Felice answered.

'Hey, what's up?'

'Sorry to call when—' she shot a glance at Simon '—you're holidaying, but you'll never guess who has shown up. I have the seventh Lord of Holm sitting across from me as we speak.'

Dead silence greeted her pronouncement. It did nothing to allay her unease. 'Felice?'

'Simon? Simon is there?'

'Uh-huh.'

'What have you told him?'

Felice's shriek nearly deafened her. She wondered if Simon could hear it from the other side of the table. He moved as if he might try and take the phone from her. Kate shifted so he couldn't. 'Nothing. Why?'

'You don't understand!'

'Obviously not.'

Simon stared at her as if he couldn't believe she had his little sister on the other end of the line. He stared at her as if he wanted to hug her. As if he wanted to kiss her in gratitude like she'd kissed that folder. All because she'd rung his little sister. Had he thought she'd leave him to stew in all that worry and concern he'd done his best to hide but couldn't?

'He will ruin everything!'

For some reason, she couldn't bring herself to believe that.

'Please, please, please, Kate. Promise me you won't tell him where I am.'

'I can hardly do that when I don't precisely know where you are myself.'

'You can't tell him I've married Danny!'

Kate bit her lip. Simon narrowed in on the action and Kate recognised the flare of desire that burst to life in his eyes. She did her best to un-bite it, but it was too late. Blood started fizzing through her veins and her mind filled with images in instant response.

Oh, stop it! He was a tourist. She didn't mess with tourists. She shook herself and forced her mind to focus on her conversation with Felice.

'Kate, promise me you won't tell him I'm married.'

Oh, dear. 'I…er…was hoping you'd do that.' She didn't want to be the one to tell Simon his sister had eloped. Amazingly, her voice was steady. Unlike her pulse.

'I will. I swear I will. I'll tell him I'm married just as soon as we get back.'

In a fortnight!

'I can just see him.' Scorn dripped from Felice's voice. 'He'll be sitting there with a frown creasing up his forehead, his chin jutting out, and he'll be drumming his fingers, just waiting for me to prove that I've done something stupid.'

Her description was so spot on that Kate had to voice her growing fear. 'Have you?'

'See?' Felice shrieked her outrage. 'He's got to you already.'

Kate didn't need to see Felice to know exactly how she'd just thrown her arm in the air or how she'd turned away only to swing back again. She put on her best employer's voice. Her boss's voice. 'Just answer the question, Felice.'

'God! You make a good pair, you know that?'

Kate shot Simon a grin. He didn't smile back. Kate pointed to the phone. 'She just said we make a good pair.'

He grinned at that.

'He really is just right there, isn't he?' Felice said.

'Yep.'

'I haven't made a mistake, Kate.'

The panic left Felice's voice. Kate blinked, averting her

gaze from Simon and his body, with all its intriguing distractions and temptations.

'I love Danny.' Felice's sincerity rang out in the quietness of her tone, and in the simplicity of her claim. 'Marrying Danny is the one good thing I've managed to do with my life.'

'Okay, okay.' Kate nodded although she knew Felice couldn't see her. 'But will you at least do one thing for me? Will you speak to Simon and tell him you're fine?'

'I don't want to speak to him.'

Kate had never heard that stubborn note in Felice's voice before. 'Please?' She held her breath.

'He'll make me hang up on him,' Felice warned.

She let out her breath. 'Nevertheless...'

'Will you promise to call me back when he's not watching over you like a guard dog?'

It was another apt description.

'Please, Kate?'

She bit back a sigh. 'Deal,' she said. Then she handed the phone across to Simon. 'Be nice,' she ordered.

He held it to his ear. 'Felice? Thank God! Are you all right?' He listened for a moment and his brow darkened. 'What the hell are you playing at? I've—'

He broke off and held the phone away from his ear. Kate wanted to tell him he wasn't doing a very good job at being nice.

He slammed the phone back to his ear. 'I've been out of my wits with worry!' His teeth clenched for a moment. 'Out with it, then,' he ordered, unclenching said teeth. 'What kind of trouble have you managed to get yourself into this time?'

In fact, he was doing a really bad job of being nice. She had a sudden flash of empathy for Felice. Felice, who was so full of life and laughter...and love.

'What do you mean, it's none of my business? I—'

Kate took a sip of her coffee and watched him. He had that over-protective big brother thing down pat. She wondered if she'd ever smothered Danny like that.

There was only five years' difference between her and Danny, though. There was ten years between Simon and Felice. Ten years. That was a lot.

'Then why the hell haven't you called?'

She set her coffee back down at that. Good question.

'You could've at least had the common decency—'

His free hand—the one not holding the phone—curved into a fist. 'Of course it's my business. I—'

The fist started to bounce on the table. 'That's rubbi   .nd you know it. I—'

He broke off to stare at the phone. He shook it, then put it back to his ear. 'Hello?' Then he turned to Kate. 'She hung up on me.'

'Of course she did.' Kate reached across and plucked her mobile from his fingers. 'I don't blame her.'

He scowled. 'You don't—'

'I told you to be nice. You weren't nice. You were bossy and…stuffy.'

He scowled some more. Then he slumped back in his chair, defeat outlined in the shape of his shoulders. 'Where is she? I'm not leaving Australia until I at least clap eyes on her.'

'Oh, right,' Kate mocked gently. 'Are you trying to tell me you'll be happy to see her in the distance, see that she's all in one piece and then leave again? I don't think so. You're itching to haul her over the coals for some imagined misdemeanour. For heaven's sake, she's twenty-two years old. Old enough to make her own decisions. Old enough to lead her own life.'

'You don't know her.' He drained his coffee in one gulp.

'I beg to differ. She's just spent the last three months living in my house, working for my business.'

His brows drew down low over his eyes. The corners of his mouth tightened. 'You don't know her like I do.'

'I'll grant you that. But you've got to stop treating her like she's twelve years old or you'll turn around one day and find out she really has done something stupid.'

His head swung up. 'Like what?'

'I don't know.' She lifted a hand and tried to pluck an example from the air. 'Like getting in with some hard and fast party crowd and taking recreational drugs or something. Just so she can prove to you she's all grown up.'

Panic raced across his face. She rushed to reassure him. 'Not that she has, you understand. I've never seen Felice take anything stronger than a glass of Chardonnay.'

He slumped back.

'But if you don't back off you could drive her to something awful and then, when she really needs you, she may not feel able to come to you.'

He dragged a hand down his face. 'The voice of experience speaketh?' he finally intoned. 'She said we made a good pair, didn't she?'

'Accused, more like.' Kate traced a finger around the rim of her coffee mug, gathered up coffee froth and popped it in her mouth. Simon's eyes narrowed as he watched her and she hastily pulled the finger away and clutched it in her lap. 'My father died eight years ago when I was twenty. My brother Danny was only fifteen.'

'Your mother?'

'She left when I was six.'

'So, basically, you raised your brother.'

It didn't sound like a question so she didn't bother answering it. 'Danny and I have had our moments, but he's only five years younger than me. It has probably been easier for me to accept that he's grown up and capable of making his own decisions.'

'Plus he's male. Men can look after themselves.'

'That's a particularly sexist view of the world.'

He shrugged, then leaned forward. 'Do you know how much Felice is worth? How much she'll inherit when she turns twenty-five?'

He named a sum that had her choking, 'What?'

He sat back and glared. 'So you can see why I'm concerned she doesn't do something stupid.'

'Like?'

His mouth grew grim. 'There's a lot of men out there who'd like to get hold of her fortune. I won't let her marry a fortune hunter.'

And then it all made crystal-clear sense to Kate—why Felice hadn't told them about her family, her fortune. She'd wanted them to love her for herself. Kate suddenly wanted to cry. She hoped Felice realised that they did love her for herself.

Something else struck her with equal force. When Simon heard about Felice's marriage to Danny, he would not share their—or her—joy.

He may well go ballistic.

He may well say unforgivable things.

Kate wanted to drop her head to the table and groan, but Simon was watching her with that direct grey gaze, so she couldn't.

'Where is she?'

The question didn't surprise her. She lifted her mug and drank the last of her coffee. This time she didn't taste it either. 'I don't know.' She set the mug back on the table.

'I don't believe you.'

'That can't be helped. I guess it's even fair enough, because even if I did know where she's staying, I wouldn't tell you.'

His mouth turned grim then. His nostrils flared. 'So that's that then, is it?'

'I'm afraid so.' A sigh of regret stole through her. 'I'm sorry, Simon, but Felice is of age and, I believe, capable of making her own decisions.'

He folded his arms and scowled.

Kate had liked the charming stranger with the to-die-for accent, empathised with the worried big brother with the clear grey eyes…but this scowling, thwarted man made her shift in her seat and wish herself elsewhere. She wondered what face he showed most often to Felice?

She recalled the panic in Felice's voice and found her answer.

And then it hit her—the scowling and the glaring; it was just a foil for his fear. It was obvious he'd spent the last few months worried sick about his sister. Instead of telling Felice he loved her and was glad she was okay, he'd lashed out at her as if…

As if he expected rejection.

What on earth had happened between them?

'What now?' he demanded. 'What the hell is she doing, anyway?'

She'd bet more people bowed and scraped to His Lordship than stood up to him. She wanted to tell him to stop acting like a spoilt child, only when she looked at him there was nothing of the child in the sensual firmness of his lips, or the broad, lean strokes of his body.

'She's seeing some of the world, back-packing like she always intended. She'll be home in a fortnight.'

'Home?' He pounced on the word. 'Her home is in England!'

Oh, dear. 'Back, then. She'll be back in a fortnight.'

Kate's back started to tighten and ache—like it always did when she felt torn. She loved Felice and had given her word. Yet it didn't stop her from feeling an enormous surge of empathy for this man sitting opposite her. She knew what it was like to fret over a sibling. She knew what it was like to worry about a child.

And Simon's expression told her he still thought of Felice as a child.

His expression also told her he needed to loosen up.

'What am I supposed to do in the meantime?' he demanded.

'You could return home to England,' she offered. 'I promise to make sure Felice calls you when she gets back.'

He shook his head once decisively. 'I'm not leaving till I see her.'

Good. Instinct told her he should stay if he wanted to mend his relationship with Felice.

'Well, then.' She gestured to the view. 'You're in the centre of a tourist Mecca, my Lord.' He was in Nelson's Bay, one of the main towns of Port Stephens—three hours north of Sydney and, in Kate's opinion, one of the prettiest places on earth. 'If you're intent on staying, have a holiday.'

'I don't have time for a holiday!'

She took in the tight set of his shoulders. 'Why not?' She might not be a doctor, she wasn't a nurse, but she had a first aid certificate and she could tell a holiday was precisely what he needed.

'I have an estate to run. I—'

'Is that more important than hanging around here and waiting for Felice?'

'No.'

Right answer. And he hadn't even hesitated. It made her lips curve into a grin. He blinked. His eyes narrowed, but she ignored his suspicion. 'Have you forgotten how to have fun? I bet all you do is work and sleep.'

And worry about Felice. She'd met men like this before. Men like her father, who thought they'd find relief in work. Hard work had helped her father up to a point. If only he'd put as much effort into winning back Kate's mother—the love of his life. Maybe then he'd have been happy.

'I—'

'You need to loosen up, Simon. You need to stop and smell the roses. Do you have rose gardens on your estate? I bet you do. Roses aren't our specialty here in Nelson's Bay, but salt is. And coconut oil.'

He stared at her as if she'd lost her mind. 'You want me to stop and smell the...coconut oil?'

'Absolutely. Everyone should stop and smell the coconut oil.'

He kept staring at her as if she'd just confirmed her craziness. Perhaps she had, but she couldn't help it—she wanted to make Simon laugh and forget his troubles like she did when Jesse came home from school glum, with the weight of the world pressing down on his seven-year-old shoulders.

'C'mon.' She stood. 'You need to feel sand between your toes and be at the centre of a lot of squawking.'

CHAPTER TWO

'I...WHAT?'

Simon stood too, but he looked far from decisive. That was okay because she'd be decisive enough for both of them. If Simon wanted to rebuild his relationship with Felice, he had to learn to loosen up. 'First things first.' She twinkled at him. 'We need to get you out of that suit.'

His eyes boggled and she had to stifle a giggle.

A giggle! For heaven's sake, she wasn't twelve. And that skippety-skip in her pulse had nothing to do with anything.

There was no denying, though, that the blood surged through her veins with a new kind of vigour.

Maybe that was a bad omen, not a good one?

She pushed the thought aside. This was about him, not her.

'I'm guessing you don't want to ruin that gorgeous Italian suit?'

'Bond Street,' he said automatically, as if he couldn't help it.

'That's a no then, is it?' She didn't wait for him to answer but tucked her hand in the crook of his elbow and tugged him towards a rack of clothes outside a nearby shop front. He was far too polite—or was that stunned—to resist.

'Ooh, end of season sales. We're in luck.' She pulled out a pair of board shorts for inspection. 'These look like they'd fit you.'

'I'm not wearing those!'

They were pink and white candy-striped. 'Pity.' She hung

them back up and pulled out another pair in loud red and yellow. She took one look at the expression on his face and shook her head. 'No,' she agreed. Then a bolt of pure mischief shook her. 'Stop press! I've found the perfect pair.' She pulled them out and held them triumphantly aloft.

Simon's jaw dropped. 'That's the Union Jack.'

'It is,' she said, eyeing them with satisfaction. 'And I think they'd suit your Lordship down to the ground.'

She suddenly found her shoulders seized in strong hands and Simon glaring down at her. His fingers curved into the soft flesh of her upper arms, firm but not hurting her. The barely contained power of the man transferred itself through his fingers to her arms…and then her brain. It made her pulse leap and jerk. For one fateful moment she thought he meant to kiss her.

If he did, she had an awful feeling she might just kiss him back.

Bad omen! Very bad omen.

'Can we drop the Lordship thing?' he growled. 'Will you please just call me Simon?'

She swallowed and nodded. 'Yes.'

He blinked as if he hadn't expected such easy acquiescence. For some reason she found that…unbelievably sad. 'I wouldn't have teased you about it if I'd known you hated it.' She had a feeling the lord thing would get right up her nose too. 'I'm sorry.'

For a moment he looked lost and she wanted to hug him.

'That's okay.'

His voice sounded hoarse, then his gaze dropped to her lips. His eyes darkened from mist-grey to charcoal. Although he didn't move a finger, his hands at her shoulders became gentler and almost seemed to cradle her. And he kept staring and staring at her lips. They tingled in response. They wanted to part, to offer him a provocative invitation.

Bad move. Reckless. But she couldn't remember the last time a man had looked at her with such naked hunger. She couldn't remember the last time a man had elicited a matching hunger from her. She couldn't remember the last time she'd been reckless.

Gloriously and wondrously reckless.

She wasn't free to be reckless.

But…

No. Not a good idea with a man who'd be gone in the blink of an eye.

'Simon?' she said, at the same time as he pulled his hands away and took a step back. She wondered if she looked as non-plussed as he did. She lifted the Union Jack board shorts, holding them up like a barrier. 'That's a no then, is it?'

He cleared his throat. 'That's a resounding no.'

'Well?' She gestured to the rack.

She watched his gaze dart along it. He pounced on a sky-blue pair. 'These will do nicely.' Then he did a double-take.

Kate started to laugh. 'I dare you to,' she challenged. The colour had obviously lulled him into a false sense of security. Overlaying the sky-blue was a Hawaiian print of golden beaches, palm trees and Hula girls. Exuberant and colourful.

Reckless.

He glared at her, raked a hand back through his too-short hair. 'I take it there's a point to all of this?'

'Absolutely.'

'And are you going to enlighten me?'

'Perhaps. It depends on how wholeheartedly you throw yourself into it.'

'Into what?'

'Ah, if you can answer that at the end of the afternoon then I'll most definitely enlighten you.'

His mouth opened and closed, but no sound came out.

'Simon—' her hands went to her hips '—do you have anything else planned for the day?'

'No, but…'

'Then just go with the flow.'

'The flow?'

Before he could think of another objection, Kate sped along to the next rack—T-shirts. 'Any preference for colour?' she tossed over her shoulder. 'And do you like a tight T-shirt or something a bit roomier?'

He was staring at her as if she'd lost her mind. Again.

She cocked her head to one side and pretended to study him, tapping a finger against her chin. 'I think you'd look great in a tight T-shirt, but for reasons of comfort I'd understand if you prefer a looser one.'

And finally he smiled.

She wanted to dance a victory jig. She didn't. She just smiled back.

'Are you always like this?'

She forced her eyes wide. 'Like what?' She handed him a shirt—blue-grey. It'd match his eyes.

'Incorrigible.'

She touched a hand to her throat in mock surprise. *'Moi?'* Then she pushed him into the interior of the shop. 'Dressing rooms are that way. If the clothes fit, leave them on. The salesman will give you a bag for your suit.'

'I—'

'And you'll need a pair of thongs.' He gazed at her in horrified incomprehension and she added, 'You know, flip-flops.' She pointed to a row of them, then turned on her heel and left him to it, her heart racing and her palms sweaty. She swiped them down the front of her shorts. Go with the flow? As long as the flow didn't contain any more thoughts of kissing and cosying up to Simon Morton-Blake, she'd be just fine.

She pulled her cell phone from her pocket.

'God! Has he gone?' Felice demanded, answering immediately and dispensing with pleasantries.

'He'll be busy for at least ten minutes, I think.'

'Please tell me you've talked him into going home.'

'You are joking, right?' Kate cast a glance back towards the menswear shop. 'I'm not even going to try. He claims he's not leaving until he sees you.'

Felice uttered something midway between a groan and a

snort. 'Don't worry, he won't hang around in Australia for a whole fortnight waiting for me to show my face.'

Kate sensed the hurt that stretched behind those words. 'We'll see.' She bit her lip. 'Want to tell me about it?'

'There's nothing to tell. Other than the fact that he's a total tyrant and too stuffy to step even a big toe out of line.'

Kate mulled that over for a moment. 'You know what? I don't think you should give a moment's notice to anything other than enjoying your honeymoon.' A girl only got one honeymoon. 'I'll take care of everything at this end, including Simon. I don't want you to give it another thought.'

'Are you sure?'

'Positive.'

'Thanks, Kate.'

Felice rang off. Kate turned to wait for Simon.

When he emerged from the shop ten minutes later, she tried to wolf-whistle, but she'd never been able to wolf-whistle to save her life. Simon was definitely wolf-whistle worthy, though. 'I've been dying to see your knees,' she teased. He had great legs—strong calves, muscled thighs...even if said legs were a tad pale. A fortnight in the sun would set that to rights.

Simon didn't smile. 'I feel like an idiot,' he grumbled.

'You look like a holiday-maker,' she returned.

Actually, he didn't. He still looked too tense and...buttoned up for a holiday-maker.

And a bit too crisp and clean.

She could set that to rights, at least.

'These are impossible to walk in.' He lifted a thong-clad foot.

'You'll get the hang of them. C'mon.'

She led him across the road, through the park and down to the beach. She kicked off her canvas tennis shoes and closed her eyes, groaning in enjoyment as she dug her feet into sun-warmed sand. Heavenly!

She kinked open one eye and found Simon staring at her in appalled fascination—thongs still on his feet and two enormous plastic carrier bags clutched in his hands. His spine was as stiff as a surfboard. She opened her other eye and shook her head. 'Simon, when was the last time you had a holiday?'

'Holiday?'

Hmm… That said it all, really. She took the plastic carrier bags from his hands and set them carefully on the beach beside her tennis shoes. 'Thongs there,' she ordered, pointing.

He complied.

'Now do this.' She twisted her body from side to side until she'd sunk up to her ankles in sand.

To his credit, Simon didn't glance around to see if anyone was watching, but followed her instructions to the letter.

'Doesn't that feel glorious?' she demanded.

'Er…yeah.'

He stared at her as if trying to work out what reaction it was she wanted. For the briefest moment her eyes stung. She wanted to yell, *Don't think about me. Do what feels good for you.*

But if he hadn't had a holiday in a long time…

'You live in Europe, right?'

'Last time I checked, England was still a part of Europe, yes.'

'Oh, ha ha, everyone's a comedian.'

He gave her a kind of half-grin. She gave him a full grin back. 'Well, Spain is nearby, isn't it? Don't you go on annual holidays to…Aruba?' She pulled the name from some dark recess of her mind.

'Kate…?'

Ooh, her name sounded divine in that to-die-for accent. She started to twist again. 'Mmm?'

'Aruba is in the Caribbean.'

Was it? 'What's a holiday destination between friends?' she said with an airy wave of her hand.

Simon threw his head back and laughed. She watched in satisfaction. She'd find the holiday-maker in him yet. Still grinning, he gazed out over the water of the bay and she recognised the flare of yearning that lit his eyes. 'Why don't you go in for a dip?'

'I don't have a towel.'

She shrugged. 'So run across the road and buy a beach towel. Or dry off after on your T-shirt.' That'd take the crispness out of it. In fact, it'd leave him deliciously rumpled.

'What about you?'

'I didn't bring my swimsuit.' She stared out at the water wistfully. 'Though I have gone swimming in shorts and T-shirt more times than I can count.' She pulled back. 'No, no. I have to go back to work in a couple of hours. I have a meeting with my accountant.' Which was a good thing, she told herself—a very good thing.

Then the scent of hot chips hit her and she forgot everything else.

Simon swung towards her when she groaned. 'Are you okay?'

'I am soooo hungry.' She pulled her feet free from the sand. 'Stay here. I'll be right back.'

It took her less than two minutes to race up to the kiosk, buy three cones of hot chips and race back.

She handed Simon one. He grinned at the two she still held. 'You weren't kidding, were you?'

'One for you, one for me and one for the seagulls.'

'One for—'

She didn't hear the rest of his sentence because she'd already thrown a chip in the air and seagulls descended from every direction to fight over it. 'Your turn.' She held the cone out to him. He took a chip and threw it. Seagulls dived and squawked. The air became alive with the flapping of wings. She laughed. He laughed. Feeding the seagulls was definitely a holiday thing. Fun.

When the cone was finished she tossed it in a nearby bin. 'These ones are mine and I'm not sharing,' she shouted to the seagulls, covering her cone with her hand. 'Come and paddle,' she said to Simon.

He blinked. 'Whilst eating chips?'

She didn't miss a beat. 'It's called alfresco dining.' She

cocked an eyebrow. 'You English lords aren't too high and mighty to get your feet wet, are you?'

'Nah,' he said, entering into the spirit, 'it's the colonials who eat with their fingers that frighten me.'

She laughed in delight. 'I didn't see you exactly rushing to bring out the silver service.'

'I'd need a table for that.' His eyes laughed down into hers. 'Not to mention a butler.'

She'd known he had to have a sense of humour. He was Felice's brother, after all.

They paddled and ate their chips. She watched the tension ease out of his shoulders, watched him lift his face to the sun.

'When was the last time you did something like this with Felice?' She tried to keep the question casual.

The tension shot back into his shoulders. His grey eyes speared hers.

'It was just a question,' she said gently. 'Instinct tells me a bit of a rift has developed between the two of you.'

He drew himself up and glared at her and, although he wore board shorts and a T-shirt, he looked as formidable as if he wore a suit of armour. 'I'm not prepared to discuss my relationship with Felice with a…'

'Stranger?' she finished for him. 'That's okay. You don't have to. Let me tell you what I think has happened instead.'

'I don't—'

'As you're ten years older than Felice,' she rushed on, talking over the top of him, 'I expect you've always felt a certain amount of responsibility for her. As Felice is ten years younger than you, I expect some time in the last few years she's rebelled against your…authority.'

She glanced at him. He didn't say anything. His lips were clamped shut, but shadows haunted his eyes.

'She's spread her fledgling wings and that's probably scared the beegeebies out of you because how on earth can you keep tabs on her when she's flitting all over the place?' She glanced at him again. He stared straight out to the front. 'The short answer, of course, is you can't. So you've become bossy and critical, she's become defiant and defensive, and suddenly, instead of having fun together, all you do is fight.'

He stopped dead in his tracks and she knew she'd struck the proverbial nail. 'You don't know me. This is all…supposition!'

Supposition that had his hands clenching into fists, she noted. 'I know Felice.' Felice was family now. She wondered how Simon would react to that news when he heard it. He glared at her. 'I know,' she agreed. 'I'm just a nosy colonial.' But her brother had married into this man's family and she wanted things to be right for Danny and Felice.

She wanted things right for Simon too.

'I think there's just enough of you in Felice for her to really get sick of your attempts to control her. Pushed too far, she'd up stumps and take off. Cut her losses.'

The colour leached from Simon's face and Kate suddenly wanted to hug him. 'But she's a nice girl at heart,' she continued, pretending not to notice his pallor. Pretending not to have noticed anything at all. 'If my hypothetical situation ever occurred, I think a heartfelt apology would go a long way towards mending fences. An apology and a promise to butt out and let her make her own decisions.' She lifted her face to the sun, welcoming its warmth. 'After all, Felice is a competent young woman, more than capable of taking care of herself.'

The colour slowly returned to Simon's face. They resumed their walk. The tension didn't leave him, but she could sense that it had subtly shifted—seemed to be directed outwards rather than inwards now.

'So,' he finally said, 'Felice has been enjoying her stay here?'

She sent him a deliberately droll look, then flung her arms wide to indicate the bay and its surrounds. 'What do you think?'

He glanced around and a reluctant grin tugged at his lips. 'I think she's probably had a ball.'

'Bingo.'

Sauntering along the water's edge like this with Simon was strangely companionable. Kate pulled in a breath, filled her lungs with air, and beneath the salt tang lay the cool, crisp scent that was Simon—wood shavings, a hint of pine and something that was purely male.

'Does your brother—Danny—live in Nelson's Bay too?'

'He does. We run the dolphin tour business together.' She glanced up at him and smiled; she couldn't seem to help it. 'My father started the business over twenty years ago.'

'And you enjoy it?'

'I love it. Most of the time.' She frowned. 'Except on those days when staff call in sick—like this morning—and I have to run around like the proverbial headless chicken to get a replacement.'

His lips twitched. 'Was that before or after the goldfish burial?'

'During.'

He was silent for a moment. 'And what do you and Danny do to have fun together?'

She tripped and almost fell flat on her face. But she righted herself almost at once and hoped her surprise didn't show. 'We share a passion for surfing and B-grade horror films. What about you and Felice?'

When he didn't say anything she nudged his arm. 'C'mon, there has to be at least one thing you guys like to do together. You have to have at least one good memory of hanging out with her.'

For heaven's sake, he was a lord. Which probably made Felice a lady. They must've had the best toys, the best holidays…the best of everything.

He straightened and glared down his nose at her. 'There are many.'

Boy, could he do haughty when he wanted to? 'Then pick a stand out,' she ordered. 'When was the last time you made her laugh? Really laugh.'

He considered her words, then a slow smile spread across his face. 'The time I taught her to walk on her hands.'

No toys. 'Where?'

'On the lawn at the Holm estate.'

No exotic location. 'When?'

His grin broadened. Kate didn't want to ask why it gladdened her heart so much.

'It would've only been five years ago.'

'Five years!' She grabbed his arm and pulled him to a stop. 'You can walk on your hands? Show me,' she demanded. 'All my life I have been trying to walk on my hands.'

So he did. He turned himself upside down and walked on his hands. His biceps bulged, the muscles in his forearms flexed, his T-shirt fell down to cover his face, and Kate's mouth watered as she took in an impeccable six-pack. He took five or six steps on his hands—Kate wasn't sure how many, she'd lost the ability to count—then he righted himself with a flourish. 'Ta da!' And then he bowed.

She stood there and gaped at him, then realised perhaps that wasn't very cool so she executed a perfect cartwheel instead.

He nodded. 'Nice.'

'I'll teach you to do a cartwheel if you'll teach me to walk on my hands.'

'I hate to break this to you, Kate, but cartwheels are a girl thing.'

'Male gymnasts do them!'

'Mmm…I'm still thinking they're a girl thing.'

'How about a back flip?' she offered. 'I can do a back flip.'

She did a back flip.

So did Simon.

And then it was on—the trying to impress each other, outdo each other. Showing off, pure and simple. Kate knew it was ridiculous and childish, but there was no denying it was fun. She laughed until her stomach ached. Then she laughed until it stopped. Finally, after another botched attempt on her part to walk on her hands, and Simon's attempt to save her, they fell to the sand in a tangle of limbs.

Kate lay back and stared up at the bluest of blue skies and tried to catch her breath. She turned her head a fraction to feast her eyes on Simon's profile. As if he could feel her gaze, he rolled to his side and propped his head on his hand. His eyes travelled over her hair, her face, and she could tell he liked what he saw. A thrill shot through her.

She tried to douse it with a dose of cold hard reality. She should pull back—turn away. Simon was a tourist. Nothing could happen between them.

'Tell me,' he started with a smile that could tempt a saint, 'exactly how scandalised would that accountant of yours be if you showed up to your meeting a tad…damp?'

She pretended to consider it. 'In all honesty, on a day like today, I expect he'll be a tad damp too.' And it wouldn't hurt her to cool off.

Simon didn't need any further encouragement. He picked her up, raced to the water's edge and tossed her in. Her laugh was cut short as water closed over her head. She bounced up, spluttering, to find him grinning and barely wet. So that was how he wanted to play it, huh? She grabbed him, hooked a leg behind his knee and dunked him.

He burst out of the water, seized her around the waist and kissed her. Hot and hard. Before she could catch her breath. Then he pulled back, but he didn't let her go and Kate knew this was what she'd been waiting for from the first moment he'd smiled at her.

He didn't move. Not forward. Not back. As if giving her a chance to pull away, to stop what was about to happen from happening.

He had to be joking, right? She wasn't going anywhere. Oh, she knew she should turn tail and run. But she couldn't… wouldn't.

One of his hands came up to cup her cheek—his eyes reflected her own confusion and wonder. Then his head dipped to hers and her lips lifted to his and she fell into him. But that seemed okay because his arms came around her and held her safe while his lips and his mouth and his tongue teased and tantalised and tempted.

Sensation spun inwards, then outwards, fizzing up through her like uncorked champagne. But still Simon held her safe. And the kiss deepened and grew until her arms twined around his neck and his hands splayed across her back, pulling her nearer, and even the gentle swell of the water propelled her closer and closer to him.

In his arms, all things suddenly seemed possible.

When Simon lifted his head, Kate didn't know if it was seconds or minutes that had passed.

'I...' He blinked, slowly, as if waking from a dream.

'Wow,' she breathed.

He grinned. A low, sexy grin. 'That's the word I was looking for.'

She eased away from him a bit because, plastered against his chest like this, she found it next to impossible to think. And she had a feeling that thinking might become crucial in the next few minutes.

'I didn't mean for that to happen,' he said, watching her carefully.

'I know.' She believed him.

'Are you...okay?' He drew back too, till they were no longer touching. Perversely, she wanted skin on skin again.

'Yes.' She wrung out her hair. Of course she was okay. She was in one piece, wasn't she? The blood might be pumping around her body with more vigour than it normally did and her lips tingling as if they'd been thoroughly kissed—which was perfectly reasonable because, of course, they had been. But the sun still shone and the seagulls still squawked and somewhere children laughed and...

Everything felt different and she didn't know why.

'Are you?' she asked. 'Okay, that is.'

'Yes.' But he drew the word out slowly as if he wasn't entirely sure and she was glad.

'What I think we should do...' she started, and his gaze shot to hers. She had to gulp back *Kiss some more* and replaced it with, 'Find a nice shady tree to dry off under.' She pointed to the strip of green beyond the beach and set off towards it without waiting for his answer.

She found a tree, sat under it and tried to talk sense into herself.

Simon lowered himself down beside her and she could feel him watching her. 'Do you want me to apologise?' he asked cautiously.

'What?' She swung to him. 'No! No, of course I don't want you to apologise.'

She wondered if his world felt turned upside down too.

'I mean, that…' she motioned to the water, to the spot where they'd kissed '…was…'

His lips twitched. 'It was,' he agreed, motioning to the same spot.

'It's just—' she turned to face him more fully, tucking her hair behind her ears '—that was just about the best kiss that I've ever had.' There was no probably about it!

He sent her another of those low, sexy grins that brought cheek creases and eye creases into play. 'There's plenty more where that came from.'

Her stomach rolled over and over on itself. Simon had hit holiday-maker mode with a vengeance and she liked it. She liked it a lot. 'Wouldn't that be reckless and irresponsible?' She deliberately used the words he'd applied to Felice.

His face grew thoughtful and he drew back. 'It would.'

'Simon, I don't do reckless and irresponsible.'

'Nor do I.'

The longer she studied him, the greater the longing that built inside her. She hadn't been with a man for a very long time, and normally she avoided any kind of romantic entanglement with tourists. Could she make an exception for Simon? The thought filtered into her mind and lodged there.

The next moment she tried to oust it. That hadn't been a holiday fling kind of kiss. It had been a…for ever kind of kiss.

She and Simon for ever?

Oh, for heaven's sake, get a grip. He lived on the other side of the world. She'd known him for a couple of hours. A sensible person did not make lifelong plans with a person they'd only known for a couple of hours. She'd obviously had too much sun. A sensible person wore a hat.

'I can see what you're thinking.'

Good God. She hoped not. She lifted her hands to her suddenly blazing cheeks. 'What's that?' she managed to croak.

'You're thinking how you hardly know me.'

'Bingo!' The heat in her cheeks started to abate. 'It's true.' She hadn't even had the benefit of getting to know him by proxy through Felice.

He reached out and took one of her hands, held it between both of his. 'It doesn't feel true.'

She knew exactly what he meant. But… 'You live a million trillion miles away on the other side of the world.' She didn't pull her hand from his.

'Well, yes…or at least ten thousand miles, but what's a trillion miles between friends, right?'

She managed a smile.

'I am, however, for the next fortnight or so based here in Nelson's Bay.' His hands tightened around hers. 'And I'd very much like to get to know you better.'

Her heart gave a joyful leap. She tried to curb it. Impossible. So she tried to talk sense instead. 'Simon, what's the point? I mean—'

He reached out and placed a finger against her lips. 'Some things don't have a point, Kate. They just are.'

His words shouldn't make sense. They shouldn't feel right.

But when he eased back and grinned at her, she grinned back and they both remained exactly where they were.

Carefully she detached her hand from his. 'So you are going to wait for Felice?'

'Yes.'

'And you want to spend the next fortnight here in Nelson's Bay?'

'That's right.'

'The room Felice was using is free at the moment,' she blurted out. 'You can use it until she returns, if you like.'

Simon drew back and stared at her. 'Stay with you…in your house?'

Good Lord, what was she doing? She gulped and swallowed and started to cough. 'I mean, that's not an invitation to…' She gestured to that spot in the water again and found it impossible to meet his eye. 'I mean, I don't do…do…'

He reached out and touched her knee, his smile kind. 'I think what you're trying to say is I'll be firmly ensconced in the guest room.'

She nodded because her throat had closed over at his touch and she couldn't speak. When he removed his hand she wanted to sigh, but whether in relief or disappointment she didn't know.

'I would be honoured to accept your hospitality. And, Kate?'

She glanced up, met the clear grey of his eyes. They'd lightened until they resembled the colour of mercury—the same colour as the bay at dawn.

'I promise I will behave like a gentleman. You can trust me.'

Could she? Yes, she had the distinct impression that she could. But could she trust herself?

'And, to thank you for your hospitality, but also because I'd very much like to, may I take you out to dinner one night soon?'

She pointed to the spot where they'd kissed. 'That can't happen again.'

He met her gaze steadily. 'It's just a dinner invitation, Kate.'

She should say no. 'I'd like that,' she found herself saying instead.

'The date ends,' he said gently, 'when you open your front door.'

It made her smile. He wanted to provide boundaries that would make her feel comfortable. She had a feeling that, despite their best intentions, one kiss would shatter those boundaries. It should make her feel wary. Instead, it fizzed her blood through her veins and made her want to throw her head back and sing.

'Are you free tomorrow night?' he asked.

Tomorrow was Saturday. Reluctantly she shook her head. 'The weekends are our busiest days on *The Merry Dolphin*.'

He frowned. 'The what?'

'My boat—*The Merry Dolphin*. Look—' she pointed '—there she is.'

She watched *The Merry Dolphin* glide through the entrance to the marina before glancing back at Simon. His jaw had dropped. 'That's your boat?'

'It is.' She couldn't contain a surge of pride. 'Lovely, isn't she?'

'Yes.'

But he was looking at her, not the boat. She tucked a non-existent strand of hair behind her ear self-consciously. 'If you like, you could spend the day on the boat with me tomorrow.'

'I'd like that. And Sunday?'

'I'm working a half day this Sunday. I should be finished by two o'clock. I'm free in the evening.'

There was that sexy grin of his again. She scrambled to her feet before she could do something stupid—like kiss him again. 'And now I have to meet with my accountant.' She needed to get away, give herself a sensible talking-to.

They arranged to meet back at her office in a couple of hours and, although she did have a long overdue appointment with her accountant, although she knew she needed to give herself a darn good talking-to, she found her feet dragging as she walked away from Simon in holiday-maker mode.

CHAPTER THREE

SIMON couldn't keep the anticipation out of his step as he turned into the arcade that led down to Kate's office. On cue, as if she'd sensed him near, she stepped out of her door and locked it.

Desire fire-balled low down in his stomach. Immediately. Without giving him time to draw breath. He stopped and feasted his eyes on her and decided breathing didn't matter. It'd kick in again when it needed to.

She was lovely. Utterly lovely. Blonde-haired and blue-eyed, lithe and strong. But it was more than how she looked. It was her essence, something innate to her, that drew him—the light in her eyes, the abandon with which she threw chips and turned cartwheels. He'd never seen the like in his life. Nobody had ever made him laugh so quickly and easily. Nobody had made him feel so accepted for who he was rather than what he was. Nobody had ever made him feel so alive.

Staying in her house, taking her out to dinner, was probably folly.

Of course it was folly.

Kate chose that moment to turn and when she saw him her whole face lit up. It made him feel ten feet tall. It made him want to sweep her up in his arms and kiss her again.

He didn't. He said, 'Did you have a good meeting with your accountant?' instead.

Boring. Predictable. Felice would take him to task over his lack of imagination.

'Yes, thank you.' Kate didn't take him to task for boringness or predictability. She smiled as if she appreciated his interest.

They stared at one another for a long moment. Simon's mouth went dry with longing. Then Kate shook her head with a laugh, took his arm and led him back the way he'd come. 'Now I'm guessing you have a hire car somewhere nearby?'

'It's just down the road a little way. Where's your car?' He tried to pull his mind back to practicalities, tried to steel himself against the light touch of her hand tucked into the crook of his arm. It fitted there so snugly he couldn't resist pulling it in against his side more securely.

'My car is stowed safely in the garage at home.' She smiled up at him and her eyes danced. 'I walk to work.'

'Good.' It meant he didn't have to let go of her just yet. It meant he didn't have to lose sight of her for even a few minutes.

'Ooh, very nice,' she said when he led her to the Mercedes E class he'd hired.

He opened the passenger door with a flourish. 'Your chariot, my lady.'

He watched her settle back against the seat and run her hands appreciatively over the leather. Mind-boggling images scorched themselves on his brain. Images of her hands running over his body like that. Images of her naked against the pale creamy leather and—

'Ooh, sat nav! Jesse is going to love this car.'

Her words snapped him back. 'Jesse?'

She glanced up and her smile widened. 'Jesse. My son.'

He closed the door. Quick and sharp. Without realising he'd meant to.

She had a child!

He stumbled around the back of the car, his movements jerky and uncoordinated as if his body didn't belong to him any more, as if gravity had taken a tighter hold on him and was trying to pull him right down through the earth.

He paused, resting his hands on his knees. A child? This lovely woman, with her wide smile and her blonde ponytail that bounced as she walked, had a child? A son?

No! He wanted to shout the denial to the sky. He'd misheard. He had to have misheard.

He forced himself upright, forced his legs forward until he stood by the driver's door, then he forced himself inside the car. He prayed his face did not betray him. 'You said you have a son?'

'That's right. He's seven and, like all boys, loves gadgets.' She rolled her eyes and gestured to the satellite navigation device. 'Didn't Felice tell you about him?'

'No.'

She turned in her seat to face him more fully. The spot between her eyes, just above her nose, crinkled. 'Simon, what exactly did Felice tell you?'

Next to nothing, or so it would seem. 'Her notes were...brief,' he admitted. Talking about Felice suddenly seemed a whole lot safer than discussing the fact that Kate had a child.

'Simon?'

He turned and met her gaze.

'When did you arrive in Australia?'

'This morning.'

Her eyes widened. 'This morning, but... Wow! You must be shattered.'

That just about summed it up.

'Well, chop-chop.' She clapped her hands. 'The sooner we're home, the sooner you can have a shower and start feeling like a normal human being again.'

Her enthusiasm—her essence—wrapped around him and he found himself smiling back at her. He couldn't help it. The woman was a witch. She was irresistible.

She had a child. His smile disappeared.

'And wait until you see the view from my back garden,' she

said as he started the car. 'It's to die for. Turn right up here at the roundabout.'

He followed her directions.

'I promise it will pep you up like nothing else. A shower, then a beer in the back garden—how does that sound?'

'Pretty good.' It did.

Except—where did her kid fit into that scenario? He tried to tell himself it didn't matter, but he knew he was lying.

'Left and then a quick right,' she said when they reached a T-junction. 'And…here it is. Home.'

She pointed to the right. Ramshackle was the first word that came to Simon's mind. He swung the Mercedes into the drive and pulled it to a halt beneath a carport attached to the double garage. Only Kate's house wasn't rundown ramshackle—it was more sprawling ramshackle. It was white weatherboard and its shape didn't conform to any style of architecture Simon had ever heard about.

Two architect-designed double-storey, cement-rendered monstrosities sat at either side—one in shades of apricot and pink, the other in blues and greys. They should've dwarfed Kate's house, but they didn't. Their windows were firmly closed to maintain air-conditioned perfection. Kate's house wasn't shut up. In fact, all the windows Simon could see were open, revealing sheer white curtains that stirred on the slightest movement of the air. In a breeze those curtains would probably flutter right out of the windows to fly like flags.

Kate grinned at him as if she could read his thoughts. The dolphin charm she wore on a silver chain around her neck glittered in the afternoon sunlight. 'It was just a tiny two-bedroom weekender with a sleep-out veranda when my father bought it. He added to it over the years.'

'It's created an…interesting effect.'

The dolphin charm suited her perfectly—graceful, strong, with just a hint of mischief. He wanted to reach out and touch the spot where it nestled in the creamy hollow of her throat.

'C'mon, I'll show you something that will really blow your mind.'

She blew his mind. And, suddenly, he didn't want her to. She had a child. He didn't want his skin tightening up whenever she smiled at him. He didn't want to notice how she walked with fluid grace as if the air were water.

And he had no business imagining what she'd look like naked. No business at all.

He grabbed her arm before she reached the front door. 'Are you married? Is there a…a father for this child of yours?'

She stared at him for a moment. Finally, she smiled. It threw him. 'Of course this child of mine has a father. It wasn't an immaculate conception, Simon. But no, I'm not married. I'm single.'

That spot between her eyes crinkled up again. 'Do you really think I would've kissed you if I was involved with someone else? Agreed to go out on a date with you? I'm aware your social circles are probably far more sophisticated than mine, but I don't appreciate what you're suggesting.'

She glanced down at the hand that encircled her arm and he hastily released her. 'No, of course not.'

She rubbed her arm at the spot where his fingers had curved around her flesh and he wondered just how tightly he'd held her. Shame hit him. 'I'm sorry.' She had been nothing but kind to him today. She didn't deserve this. 'I just…'

'Panicked?'

He thought about that, then nodded. 'Yes.'

She smiled at him again. 'Crazy.'

The whole day had been crazy. Thoughts of him and this woman together the craziest of all. But they did have a fortnight. And, if she was willing… After all, the child had to go to bed at some time, didn't he?

Something about that thought seemed off kilter. He dragged a hand down his face. He'd think about it tomorrow, after he'd had a decent night's sleep. At the moment, no matter how hard he tried, he couldn't seem to form a sensible thought to save himself.

Kate led him through the house via a crooked, higgledy-piggledy hallway to a double glass sliding door at the back. She pulled it open and stepped outside. 'There.' She flung her arms wide. 'What do you think?'

Simon forced his gaze from the tempting curves and delights of her body, from the ravishing vision of having those arms wrapped around him, and forced his eyes to the view she indicated.

He blinked and sucked in a breath. When he let it out again a sense of calm—totally at odds with the storm raging through him moments before—descended over him.

'Amazing, isn't it?' she whispered.

'Utterly.' He found himself speaking quietly too, not wanting to break the stillness, the sense of tranquillity. He couldn't remember the last time he'd felt so at peace.

'When she first saw this view, it was one of only two times I ever saw Felice at a loss for words.'

He could understand that. Spread out before them, calm and smooth, touched with orange and gold as the sun started to set, was a bay as wide as he'd ever seen. The view was unimpeded all the way out to the sea horizon. Below them was a strip of green—a park lined with gums and flame trees—and, beyond that, away to the right, a strip of white beach.

'What was the second?'

'The second what?'

She didn't turn to meet his gaze, but continued to gobble up the view, to guzzle it as if it renewed her somehow, topped up the reserves the day had depleted. Simon suddenly wished he'd left the question unasked, that he'd left her to enjoy her view in peace.

'Second what?' she repeated, glancing at him.

'The second time you saw Felice at a loss for words?'

Her eyes became gentle at some memory, but she shook her head. 'That isn't a story for today. I'll leave Felice to tell it.'

'Mum!'

Simon swung around to find a sandy-haired boy racing

towards them from the garden next door. When he glanced back at Kate, a smile lit her face with so much joy it stole his breath.

The child flung his arms around her waist. 'I got a six! I got a six!'

'Woo hoo!'

Simon blinked as he watched them do a victory dance. At least that was what he figured the tangle of limbs and jumping in the air was meant to indicate.

'And I clean bowled two of them!'

They performed more victory dancing. Over Jesse's head Kate grinned at him, completely oblivious to his consternation—for which he was grateful.

'Jesse is cricket mad,' she explained.

Then she waved to someone who stood on the deck of the house next door. 'Thanks, Flora. I hope he wasn't any trouble.'

'None at all. He and Nick keep each other occupied.'

Good Lord—there was another child? He could tell at a glance that this one wasn't Kate's, though.

With a wave, Flora and the child disappeared back inside their house.

'Flora minds Jesse for me most afternoons. Just for an hour or so until I get home.' She cuddled her son close. 'And this, of course, is Jesse.'

An ache thumped to life in Simon's chest and was echoed behind his eyes. Why did mothers always expect a person to find their children adorable?

'Jesse, this is Felice's brother…'

She glanced up at him expectantly. He shifted his weight from one foot to the other, not sure what she expected from him. Most of his friends kept their children firmly hidden. Which suited him just fine.

'Would you prefer Simon or Mr Morton-Blake?' she started slowly, as if he were a child too. Her eyes suddenly danced mischief. 'Or Lord—'

'Simon will be fine,' he cut in quickly.

He stared at Jesse. Jesse stared back at him. Then, because he didn't know what else to do, and Kate quite clearly expected something from him, he shot out his hand towards the child. 'I'm pleased to meet you.'

Jesse's eyes widened. He pressed into his mother's side, but when she nudged him he reached out to shake Simon's hand.

Simon gripped the child's hand briefly. Then let it go. Fast. Children were so small and vulnerable, so noisy and destructive. And he didn't want anything to do with this one.

'I...um...would it be all right if I took that shower now?'

'Of course.'

Kate beamed at him. It made the ache in his chest and behind his eyes thump harder.

'I'll show you your room.'

'You have your own bathroom,' Jesse said, trailing into the house after them.

Simon glanced back at him uneasily, then rolled his shoulders. 'Excellent,' he managed. At least he wouldn't run into this pint-sized pocket of energy in that particular room of the house.

Kate opened one of the doors off the higgledy-piggledy hallway. 'Here it is.' She stood aside to let him enter, then pointed. 'En suite is through that door there.'

'Thank you.'

'We'll be back down that way in the kitchen or family room—' she hitched her head in the direction they'd come '—when you're finished.'

'Okay.'

'Oh, and I'd better grab you a towel.'

She disappeared back down the hallway. Jesse followed her and Simon heard him ask, 'Is he really Felice's brother?'

'He sure is.'

'Cool!'

It was Jesse who reappeared clutching a fluffy white bath towel. 'Here you go.' He handed it to Simon shyly.

Simon took it. 'Thank you.'

'Do you play cricket?'

Simon didn't know what to say so he opted for the truth. 'Yes.' Then, because he didn't know what else to do, he closed the door in the child's face.

The shower made him feel cleaner, but not back to normal. He turned the heat up as far as he could stand it before finishing with a blast of cold. For penance. Only he couldn't remember what he was paying penance for. He dragged the towel over his hair and scrubbed until his scalp tingled. A good night's sleep—that was all he needed. He'd feel right again tomorrow.

He found Kate—and Jesse—in the open-plan kitchen and family room, just as she'd promised. He remembered another promise. Something about a beer in her back garden. He caught sight of her perky ponytail and anticipation inched through him.

'Good shower?' She glanced up from slicing salad vegetables.

'The best,' he said because the sight of her had his gut clenching with the desire to make her smile.

'Simon plays cricket,' Jesse announced to nobody in particular as far as Simon could tell.

Kate set her knife down and sized Simon up with her glorious baby-blues. 'Ah…but can he play it well? That's the question. Can he play better than Felice?'

'Uh-huh.' Jesse nodded. 'I bet he plays for England. You do, don't ya, Simon?'

Kate folded her arms, her lips twitching. 'England, huh? C'mon, Simon, 'fess up now. Don't be shy. Do you play for crown and country?'

'Um…no.' He shoved his hands in his pockets.

Jesse squinted up at him. 'Who do you play for then?'

Jesse's gaze had been glued to Simon's face since Simon had entered the room, although he had done his level best to ignore it.

'This is third degree time,' Kate said kindly, scooping up

freshly sliced lettuce and cucumber into a salad bowl before dragging a bag of tomatoes towards her chopping board.

He didn't want to be third degreed.

'Ooh, Jesse,' she suddenly crooned, taking her knife up again, 'you should see Simon's car. It's gorgeous. Sat nav and everything.'

'Wow!' Jesse gazed at Simon hopefully.

No way. Cars weren't toys and kids were destructive. They didn't watch where they were going. They broke things—like satellite navigation devices. With his luck, the boy would knock the car out of gear or something. Slam his thumb in the car door.

No way.

He kept his mouth firmly shut and his feet firmly planted. He would not offer to show him the car. Kate sent him a puzzled glance. He shoved his hands deeper into his pockets. 'Didn't you say something about a beer in your back garden?'

Her frown cleared. With a low laugh, she pointed. 'Beers are in the fridge. Help yourself. I'm going to be tied up in here for another half an hour. I'll join you when I'm finished.'

'I'll wait.' Sitting out there on his own...or, worse still, with the child...held little appeal.

The smile she sent him seared him from the toes up and made him glad he'd offered to wait. She had a luscious mouth, lips full and soft. When he'd kissed her she'd tasted of sunshine and lemonade—the homemade variety, not the fizzy stuff.

He wanted to kiss her again.

And again. And again.

He wanted to kiss her and not stop.

'Simon!'

He came back to earth with a crash when he realised those full lips were directing words at him. 'Sorry?'

She swallowed. He took in the high colour on her cheek-bones and couldn't hold back a grin. He remembered the way she'd wound her arms around his neck and kissed him back. He wanted to grab her around the waist and whirl her around in a victory dance of their own. He didn't, but his grin widened. 'I was miles away.'

Her mock glare told him she knew exactly where he'd been. Then she glanced at Jesse. Simon shuffled from one foot to the other and bit his tongue to stop him from asking when Jesse went to bed.

'I was saying,' she started with exaggerated care, 'that you play cricket…'

'That's right.'

'And Jesse plays cricket…'

'Uh-huh.'

'Then maybe the two of you would like to go down to the beach and have a quick game while I finish tossing the salad and get the casserole on?'

The blood drained from his face. Ice pierced his veins. He took a step back. 'No!'

If something happened to Jesse whilst he was in Simon's care, Simon would never forgive himself.

Kate would never forgive him.

Her head shot up. She stared at him as if she couldn't believe she'd heard him properly, then she very slowly set the knife down on the chopping board. With sickening clarity, he recognised each and every emotion that passed through her eyes—concern, shock, consternation, disappointment and finally…anger.

Then her eyes became as opaque as frosted glass and she turned away from him.

'Oops, that's right, chook. You won't have time for a game of cricket this afternoon. Not if you and Nick want to camp out in the tent tonight.'

Jesse's face lit up. He flung his arms about her waist. 'Can we?'

Kate hugged him close. 'Sure you can.'

Bitterness filled Simon's mouth. Kate and Jesse formed a closed circle, effectively shutting him out. Even though he knew he deserved it, and even though he knew it was for the best, the bite of their rejection seared through him like poison.

Kate hugged Jesse close, giving him the reassurance he needed after Simon's abrupt rebuff. Then she said, 'Why don't you run over and make sure it's okay with Nick's mum?'

Jesse shot out the back door, everything right with his world again, and Kate spun to Simon. 'What on earth was that about?' she demanded, her hands going to her hips.

She wanted to hit him. She wanted to kiss him too, but she tried to ignore that bit. She tried to focus on her sense of injury. How could he have been so darn brutal? Jesse was a great kid. He hadn't deserved that.

Simon hunched up his shoulders and shrugged. She tried not to notice how long and lean his legs looked in sand-coloured chinos, tried to ignore the broad strokes of his chest and shoulders in their forest-green polo shirt.

Okay, well, maybe it was impossible to ignore them, but they didn't excuse his behaviour.

'Well?' she demanded.

He shrugged again. 'Look, Kate, I'm just not that into children, that's all.'

'Not into kids?' That's all?

'Look, it's no big deal.'

No big deal?

That's all!

With those few words, Simon dismantled all the castles in the air she'd built around him since that kiss—that stupid, ridiculous kiss. They fell around her like they deserved to— silently and strangely weightless—whilst she tried to get her head around the extent of her own stupidity.

All her adult life she and her friends had warned each other—don't mess with the tourists. And here she was messing with the worst kind—the kind that kissed you senseless, made you fall in love with them, took all you had to offer, then buggered off back to wherever it was they'd come from without so much as a backward glance. Well, this little black duck wasn't falling in love with anyone! Not this week.

One—love at first sight was a myth.

Two—hot, steamy kisses did not indicate a warm heart or a good person or anything else of the kind.

Three—Jesse's happiness took priority over all else. Not that she was in any danger of forgetting that, but it felt good to tell herself all the same.

And four—don't mess with the tourists!

Simon shifted from one foot to the other. 'You're not all right with that, are you?'

She stared at him. Her hands clenched and she started to shake. 'You have no idea how *not* all right with that I am. I am so *not* all right with it that I want you to forget all about taking me out to dinner on Sunday night.'

He stiffened. 'But I've already booked at—'

'I don't care if you've organised dinner with the Queen!'

'All because I'm not into children?'

'That's right.' She gave one hard nod.

'But you and me…can't we keep that separate—?'

'Separate!' She advanced on him. 'You have no idea, do you?' Then she had to retreat before she did something stupid like cry.

'But—'

'Face facts,' she ordered, as much to herself as him. 'You're not into kids and I have one. I'd say that's a pretty major problem from the outset, wouldn't you?'

She seized a tomato and ordered herself not to squash it. 'Me and Jesse, we're a package deal. End of story.'

Simon took a step back.

'Precisely!' She nodded. Then she picked up her knife and very carefully set about chopping the tomato. When Simon turned and left the room, she refused to waste another moment thinking about him. Not one more thought.

* * *

Kate tried to keep things as normal as she could for the rest of the afternoon. Once she'd finished preparing dinner, she, Jesse and Nick put up the tent.

Eventually Simon emerged out of hiding to sit at the outdoor table. She set a beer in front of him. He murmured his thanks, but he didn't offer to help with the tent.

Not that she, Jesse and Nick needed any help.

She kept up a steady flow of chatter during dinner—again, mostly with Jesse and Nick. She tossed the occasional comment to Simon, but each time she did he'd have to rouse himself and she'd have to repeat what she'd said. In the end she left him to himself.

Which suited her just fine.

A more charitable part of her knew he must be jet lagged. If she'd flown into Sydney from London this morning, jumped straight into a hire car to drive three hours north and had then spent a couple of hours doing handstands and back flips on the beach, she'd be jiggered.

He'd do handstands with her on the beach, but he wouldn't spare her son even half an hour to play cricket? What kind of Jekyll and Hyde did that make him?

What kind of idiot did that make her? What on earth had possessed her to offer him Felice's old room? She wanted to take that offer back now, tell him to find some fancy hotel to book into. She wanted to forget how he'd made her feel like a princess in a fairy tale—beautiful, desired...at the centre of his world. It was hard to forget when he sat across the table from her.

The more rational part of her brain told her that kicking him out might be construed as a wee bit of an overreaction. He and Felice needed to sort out whatever it was they had to sort out. Build bridges. Mend fences. Instinct told her that would be important to Felice. Which would make it important to Danny. Which made it important to her.

Besides, kicking Simon out would mean admitting she'd placed too much importance on that kiss.

And she didn't. Not now. She'd read more into it than she should have, that was all.

But as she stared across at Simon, she couldn't remember the last time she'd got someone so wrong.

'Are you really going to let them sleep out here all night on their own?' Simon asked when Jesse and Nick dived into the tent with Game Boys, popcorn and torches.

It was the longest sentence he'd uttered since their set-to in the kitchen.

'They won't last past nine-thirty out here. They'll freak each other out with ghost stories and end up in their sleeping bags on the lounge room floor. Why? Do you have a problem with children camping out?'

Stupid question. He had a problem with children full stop.

He shrugged, shifting on his seat. 'I just thought it might be dangerous, that's all.'

The sun had finally set and light from the house threw shadows across his face. It was hard to read his expression. 'Dangerous how?'

'I don't know.' He grimaced, clearly uncomfortable. 'A tree could fall on the tent, they could get bitten by a spider, a stranger could take them.'

'Any of those things could happen in broad daylight,' she pointed out.

He shoved his chair back and shot to his feet. 'I'm going to bed.'

He stalked into the house and Kate did not call a cheery goodnight after him. She didn't trill, *Don't let the bedbugs bite.* She didn't tell him what time to set his alarm or what time they were having breakfast. No sirree. She kept her mouth well and truly shut. She'd opened her heart to him a little too quickly, a little too widely, earlier in the day. She had to find a way to close it again.

And keeping her mouth shut seemed a good place to start.

CHAPTER FOUR

SATURDAY dawned as golden and blue as the previous day. When Simon opened his eyes, the sunlight spilling in through the open window and across his bed melted the mist that had held him in thrall last night. All in one blink of his eyes.

He could not mess around with Kate Petherbridge.

Not for a casual holiday fling and not for anything longer term.

Jeez! He shot up and scrubbed both hands down his face before scratching them back through his hair. Definitely not for anything longer term.

He tossed the covers back, sat on the edge of the bed and cradled his head in his hands. He didn't mess with single mothers.

Yesterday, down at the beach, the strange magic that had surrounded him for a while…he had to put that out of his mind. Put it down to relief at discovering Felice was okay, and the culture shock of finding himself on a warm beach in summer with a woman who didn't care a jot about his title, about dignity, and who smiled as if she had sunshine in her soul.

It had all gone to his head.

A good night's sleep had sorted him out, though. He'd be okay again now. But as he rose to walk to the shower he couldn't remember the last time he'd been so aware of his body—how strongly the blood pumped through his veins, how deeply he could fill his lungs, how tall he could stretch. This

Nelson's Bay of Kate's seemed as magical and exotic as an Aladdin's cave—a place that only existed in the imagination.

Simon pushed the thought out of his mind. He didn't believe in fairy tales. No matter how hard the sun shone, today's reality was dull, grey and unyielding.

He didn't mess with single mothers.

He reminded himself of that fact fifteen minutes later when he made his way to the kitchen. Then he promptly forgot it.

Kate and Jesse sat at the table, haloed in all of their blonde glory by the morning sunlight that spilled into the room at every window. In fact, the room was more window than wall. It made him blink, but Kate and Jesse, faces alive with animation and at home in the sunlight, chattered away to each other about…birds? Simon had never wanted to sit himself down and join a conversation with as much hunger as he did now.

The chattering abruptly stopped. Two faces turned to the doorway as one, as if they'd sensed him there at the same time, both faces wary. Kate's wary *and* shadowed, as if she hadn't slept.

'Good morning,' she said, but her lips didn't lift into yesterday's ready smile.

'Good morning,' Jesse said, following her lead.

He had a feeling that as far as children went, Jesse was a good one. Which was another reason Simon had best keep his distance. 'Good morning,' he managed in return.

Kate pointed to the breakfast bar and an array of cereal boxes. 'Help yourself. There's bread in the breadbox for toast. Coffee's in the pot.'

'Thank you.'

Then she promptly turned back to Jesse and resumed their conversation, excluding him. Simon's stomach filled with acid. Yesterday, for a while there with this woman he'd felt a part of something bigger than himself. It had probably been a mirage—a product of jet lag and relief…and a kiss that had blown his mind.

He rolled his shoulders and glanced at Jesse. He had to forget about that kiss. He didn't want to be a part of something this big.

He poured himself a coffee, hesitated at one end of the kitchen table, but as Kate and Jesse's conversation skittered to another halt and Kate's shoulders stiffened, he forced his legs to carry him all the way to the sliding glass door and outside to the shabby but obscenely comfortable outdoor setting.

For some reason this eclectic collection of chairs around a scuffed wooden table—round so nobody sat at the head—made him smile. He'd seen enough of Kate's remarkable home to know she wasn't the kind of woman who would fit in at Holm House. He had a feeling she'd despise the fuss accompanying valuable antiques, the exaggerated care taken not to scratch or damage them, and the painstaking restoration of fabrics for sofas as stiff and uncomfortable as stone. Kate's house was feet-up-on-the-furniture comfortable.

It suddenly occurred to him that in his private apartments he didn't need to put up with the antiques either.

Kate stuck her head around the door and anticipation fired along each and every nerve-ending before he could stamp it out. If only she'd sit down with him for a minute…

'If you still want to come out on *The Merry Dolphin* today—'

'I do.' The words shot out of him too quickly, but he couldn't hold them back. He couldn't mess with her. He couldn't kiss her or make love with her—his skin tightened at the thought— or flirt with her or try to woo her or do any of the things his body urged him to do. But at least he could go out on her boat.

'Then we leave in half an hour.'

'I'll be ready,' he promised.

She glanced at his mug of coffee and he waited for her to tell him he should eat something, but she didn't. She disappeared back inside and she hadn't smiled. Not once.

'Ready?'

Simon leapt up from the outdoor table. 'Yes.' He followed Kate and Jesse down to the bottom of the garden to a set of wooden steps he hadn't noticed earlier. They led down into a park lined with flame trees and jacarandas, and around to a perfect crescent of golden sand.

Simon's steps faltered as he took in a picturesque sheltered bay. 'This is…' he glanced back the way they'd come to see if he could glimpse a cave sparkling with gold and gems, and turbaned men whizzing around on magic carpets '…amazing.'

'This is Dutchman's Beach,' she said, matter of fact. Jesse raced down to the beach. She kept to the path and didn't lead him down to the sand. 'Around the point is the marina, which is where we're headed. Further around are Nelson's Bay, then Little Beach where we—'

Everything inside him stiffened. He waited for her to say, kissed. The kiss grew shockingly vivid in his mind—the feel of this woman in his arms, the silk slide of her skin against his palms, the trembling of her lips beneath his and the taste of her.

'Where we were yesterday.'

Her voice wobbled and he knew she remembered too. Then he remembered the things she'd said to him afterwards and a weight crashed down on his shoulders.

'Large portions of the bay are a wildlife sanctuary,' she continued, her voice determined now, with not a wobble to be heard.

Simon found it hard enough to walk in a straight line let alone talk too. He stared ahead at Jesse and told himself he could not kiss Kate.

'For example, you're not allowed to fish off the marina or the beach at Nelson's Bay, and it's forbidden to collect shells and seaweed along here at Dutchman's.'

Just like it was forbidden for him to kiss her.

Kate continued her spiel, as if she'd memorised it for this precise purpose. He couldn't focus on fishing and seaweed or environmental preservation. He concentrated on keeping his hands at his sides and prayed he made the appropriate sounds in all the appropriate places.

'Watch your step,' she called over her shoulder as she boarded *The Merry Dolphin*. Simon swore they both breathed a sigh of relief that they'd made it to their destination. The water in the marina was so calm he barely noticed the difference between pier and boat. He followed her past a steep set of stairs and down a short corridor to a generously proportioned lower deck.

'Guess what, Mum.' Jesse sat on the counter of a small two-sided bar. 'Uncle Archie caught a snapper this big yesterday.' He held his arms wide.

From the size of Jesse's eyes, Simon guessed he liked fishing almost as much as cricket.

'Very impressive,' Kate said.

A grizzled, grey-haired man stood behind the bar.

'Archie, this is Simon, Felice's brother.'

The two men shook hands.

'Archie is my business partner. He and my father started the dolphin tour business over twenty years ago,' she explained, but she didn't look at him as she did so.

'Did you use your new rod?' Jesse asked. 'Did you take a photo?'

'Sure I did. It's upstairs. Wanna take a look?'

When Jesse nodded, Archie lifted him down from the bar and, with a wink in Simon's direction, ushered the child back the way Simon and Kate had just come and up the steep staircase. Kate immediately moved behind the bar and started stocking the refrigerator.

Simon stared at the spot where Archie and Jesse had been and then to the stairs. He scowled. He scuffed the floor with his shoe. Archie had that knack with kids that Simon utterly lacked.

Not that he'd tried to cultivate it. Experience told him not to bother.

'Are you okay, Simon?'

He swung back to find Kate staring at him with a frown in her eyes and cans of soda clutched in her hands. 'Yes.' He settled his customary mask back into place. 'Nice boat.' He forced himself to glance around its interior. Then he did a double-take. 'God, Kate! How big is this thing?'

'*The Merry Dolphin* is nineteen point eight metres.' And for the first time that day a glimmer of a smile hovered on her lips. He watched, he waited, he held his breath, but it didn't break free. He dragged his gaze away, not wanting thoughts of kissing her to take over his mind again. He focused on the boat instead.

The bar stood on his left and on the right was a nook for making tea and coffee. Polished wood and brass shone in the sunlight pouring in at the windows. The wood-panelled walls gleamed, the windows sparkled and the rich brown of the carpet was reassuringly springy beneath his feet. Two rows of tables and chairs created an avenue down the centre of the lower deck leading to a small ladder and a pair of open glass doors that stretched out to the foredeck.

He took a step forward and tried to take it all in, spun slowly on the spot. He couldn't wait to see the view from here when they were out in the middle of the bay. He opened one of the windows. The water was so close he could stretch down and touch it, so clear he could see to the sand and rocks below. 'Wow.' He swung back to Kate. 'Felice would've loved this.'

Kate's glimmer became a full-blown smile. 'She did.'

He knew the smile was for Felice, but it kicked him in the gut all the same. It kicked him harder when the smile faded and the wariness returned to her eyes.

'Hiya, Kate.'

Kate swung to the man who'd just jumped on board. 'Hiya, Pete.' She turned back to Simon. 'Pete is our third crew member for the day. Pete, this is Simon, Felice's brother.'

'Hi.' Pete nodded at Simon, his grin broad. 'Is that Jesse upstairs?'

'It is.'

With another nod, Pete shot upstairs too.

Simon swallowed, rolled his shoulders. 'So you need three people to crew *The Merry Dolphin*?'

'Through the week we manage with two, but on school holidays and weekends I like to have a third person to help out with all the kids.'

He had a feeling she'd said that deliberately. She'd certainly said it with relish.

'We need someone to keep an eye on them in the boom nets.'

He gazed at her blankly. 'The boom what?'

She gestured for him to follow her outside. She pointed to the nets stretched between metal frames attached to the boat—one at the back, one to the side. 'We lower them in the water and take the kids for a ride.'

Simon's jaw dropped. 'Isn't that dangerous?' He couldn't keep the note of accusation out of his voice.

She rolled her eyes. 'You are such a killjoy.'

He shoved his hands in his pockets. There were worse things to be.

'The kids love it.'

He just bet they did. He made a mental note to stay away from the back of the boat whenever the boom nets were down. He made a mental note to stay away from the kids.

He pushed the images out of his mind. 'I thought you said Danny worked with you.'

'He does.' She bustled back inside and refused to look at him again.

'But he's not here today?' He didn't know why he pressed the point—what was it to him if her brother had the day off? He just wanted her to keep talking to him.

'Danny is on holiday.'

She went back to stocking the refrigerator but, as far as Simon could tell, the refrigerator was already bursting at the seams. He leant on the bar to watch her.

'He works full on during the school holidays on the under-standing that he can take two weeks off as soon as they're over,

so he can go on surfing holidays up the coast with his mates.'
She rose and wiped her hands down the front of her trousers. 'He
left on Wednesday. He'll probably be back before you leave.'

She still wouldn't look at him. Ice started circling his scalp.
Felice was on holidays…

'When did Felice leave?'

Kate stuck her chin out. 'Wednesday too.'

Danny was on holiday… His heart started to thump. 'Danny
and Felice, are they…?'

She folded her arms and raised an eyebrow. 'Are they
what…? Dating? Absolutely. They're very close.'

He wanted to reach out and shake her. 'You didn't see fit to
tell me this yesterday?'

'No more than you saw fit to tell me you weren't into
children,' she shot back. 'And why's that? Because down at the
beach yesterday it didn't seem all that important, did it?'

She was right. He shifted his weight. 'How old is Danny?'

'Twenty-three.'

Relief poured into him. Twenty-two and twenty-three—it
wouldn't be more than some holiday fun.

Jesse, Archie and Pete clambered back down the stairs.

'Time,' Archie intoned.

'Oh!' Kate glanced at her watch and grabbed a clipboard
from beneath the bar. 'Roll call,' she explained to Simon. 'You
want to pilot first?' she called out to Archie.

'Nah, it's all yours. I'll take first shift on the bar.' He glanced
at Simon. 'I might even put this brother of Felice's to work and
see how he stacks up.'

'How are your tea and coffee making skills?'

Her raised eyebrow told him she doubted they'd be up to
scratch.

'Excellent.' If he spent the day making tea and coffee would
she finally smile at him?

'Good, because we have about forty people booked for our
first tour. They'll keep you busy.'

He couldn't help but follow her back outside.

She pointed to the steps. 'Now would be a good time to check out the upper deck if you wanted to.'

Then she leapt down to the pier with all her easy grace and all Simon was left with was the scent of her and the creaking of the boat.

He took the steps up. The top deck boasted three-hundred-and-sixty-degree views. A fibreglass roof canopy provided shade. Padded benches that ran around the sides provided the only seating but six floor-to-ceiling poles provided anchorage points for those who wanted to stand. He moved to stand beside the wheel and controls and imagined Kate there, looking ship-shape and perfect.

Laughter and voices drifted up to him. He glanced down and was caught by the sight of Kate. Kate in the sun with her blonde ponytail shining and a smile on her face as she welcomed her passengers. He stared at her for a long moment, then made his way back downstairs and took up a station beside Archie at the bar for the first dolphin tour of the day.

At the end of the first tour, Kate and Jesse jumped down to the pier. Simon wanted to follow them but something in the set of Kate's shoulders warned him not to.

It was the same something that had kept him at arm's length all morning. Dammit! He knew he couldn't kiss her, make love with her or flirt with her, but couldn't she at least smile at him? He was still the same guy she'd joked around with yesterday, even if he wasn't any good with children.

He couldn't stop his eyes from following her. In the strong midday light, she gleamed golden and navy. Navy—the colour of her uniform of cropped linen trousers and polo shirt with *The Merry Dolphin* emblem embossed on the pocket. Golden—the colour of her hair, her skin…her smile.

And she was smiling, he realised with a start, but it sure as hell wasn't at him. The person she smiled at was some blond, muscular surfer type who grinned and waved as she strolled towards him. Anger he didn't understand clenched Simon's gut.

Jesse raced up to the man and was swung up in a hug. From where he stood behind the bar, Simon could hear Jesse's laughter.

Jesse's father?

It wasn't relief that poured through him, though. Not when the man bent down and planted a kiss on Kate's golden cheek and gave her a one-armed hug. Simon leant his forearms on the bar and clenched his hands, fought the urge to pulverise this blond, muscular surfer type who looked so bloody... *perfect*...beside Kate.

'That there's Paul,' Archie said.

He glanced down at Simon's hands. Simon straightened and shoved them in his pockets.

'He's Jesse's dad. Nice bloke.'

Simon nodded. He couldn't manage anything else. He had no right to this possessiveness, this...jealousy. But knowing it and making himself feel it, he found, were two very different things.

'Kate and Paul are good friends.' Archie's faded blue eyes considered Simon shrewdly. 'But there isn't anything between them now. Hasn't been for a long time.'

Simon gave a terse, 'It's none of my business.'

'Is that so?' The older man chuckled. 'Seems to me you're wishing mightily that it were.'

Simon stared out at Kate, Paul and Jesse. What was the word she'd used yesterday?

Bingo?

Tour Two. Simon gritted his teeth. How much tea and coffee did a guy have to make before he'd earned one measly smile?

Fair enough, on that first tour when he'd been downstairs and Kate had been upstairs—he'd spent that tour concentrating on the running commentary she'd given through the PA system.

He'd lost himself in identifying the different tones of light and shade in her voice.

But they were halfway through the second tour now and she and Archie had switched places. She was standing right beside him behind the bar and she wouldn't even look at him, let alone smile at him. She didn't even have the excuse of thirsty customers at the moment. The passengers were all too busy staring out of the windows, oohing and aahing over dolphins.

She filled his vision and yet she wouldn't even spare him a smile.

'You certainly like to give a guy the silent treatment when you're ticked off with him, don't you?'

The words burst out of him and when her jaw dropped a grim satisfaction threaded through him. Any reaction was better than none.

She tried to edge away, but there wasn't much room for edging behind the bar. So she folded her arms and glared at him instead. 'I'm not ticked off.'

He snorted. 'Then I'd hate to see the real thing.'

He wanted to seize her by the shoulders and shake her, order her to smile. He pinched the bridge of his nose between forefinger and thumb. Why the hell did it matter so much?

She gestured to the speakers. 'I thought you might like to listen to Archie's commentary.'

'Why on earth would I want to do that? I listened to yours, didn't I? I know we're heading around into Shoal Bay, that across the way is Hawkes Nest and Tea Gardens. I know dolphins have a life span of forty to forty-five years and that they eat six to eight kilos of fish a day!'

She blinked.

He wanted to smash his hand down on the bar between them. If he'd just played cricket with Jesse yesterday she'd be laughing and smiling and joking with him now. She might even have let him kiss her again.

If only he'd played cricket with Jesse...

The blood in his veins turned to ice. He could not have played cricket with Jesse. Not on the beach. Not on his own. It was pointless pretending otherwise.

He put the thought away. She was right to pull back from him.

'Excuse me, mate, but you wouldn't happen to know the latest test score, would you?'

A passenger—in his mid-sixties, Simon guessed—had sidled away from his wife to shoot the question out the corner of his mouth.

'Don't ask him.' Kate's voice dripped with scorn. 'He wouldn't have a clue. He doesn't even like cricket.'

Yes, he did. Just because—

'Ricky Ponting is only eight runs off his ton,' she said, flipping out her cell phone and glancing at the screen. 'The Aussies are four for two hundred and ninety-seven.' She snapped it shut again. 'Looks like we're going to post a nice total.'

'Cheers, love.' The man shot her a grin and with a thumbs-up sidled back over to his wife.

'That wasn't fair,' Simon spluttered.

'No?' She raised a mock-concerned eyebrow. 'Sorry, my mistake.'

She turned away, clearly dismissing him. Again. He closed his eyes, dragging in a breath, and that was when her scent hit him. She smelt like sunflowers. Against a backdrop of sea, salt and coconut-scented sunscreen, it was strangely erotic. It drenched his senses, soaked through his skin and into his blood. His stomach dissolved. Other parts of him started to harden. His mouth went dry.

He forced his eyes open again. He had to get a grip. 'Look,' he managed to grind out, 'I'm sorry I didn't play cricket with Jesse yesterday, all right? But I had phone calls to make and emails to send. I run an estate. It's not like my absence won't go unnoticed. I had to make…arrangements.'

He knew he was making excuses. He just hoped she'd buy them.

'Phone calls that couldn't wait for half an hour?' she snapped without turning around.

'And I was jet lagged.' He was fighting a losing battle.

She swung back then, hands on hips. 'Fine! But Jesse didn't see it that way.'

He straightened. How the hell was he supposed to read some child's mind? She looked as if she wanted to take a swipe at him. She looked gorgeous. He gave in. 'How did Jesse see it?'

'He loves Felice. He and Felice play cricket and football on the beach all the time. He just wanted to have a laugh with her brother, that's all.'

He shoved his hands in his pockets. He didn't understand children at all, and this just went to prove he should stay well away from them.

'But you know what, Simon? It's not the fact that you wouldn't play cricket with Jesse.'

Now he wasn't getting her either.

'It's the way you turned him down!'

The way he'd…

She poked him in the chest, her frustration clear, but the moment her finger connected with him, she stilled. He stilled. He watched the way her eyes travelled over his chest and everything inside him clenched.

'Kate!'

She pulled her hand away, stepping back as far as the dimensions of the bar would allow, but the things inside him didn't unclench. When he met her eyes, those things inside him clenched even harder. She wanted him. Still. She was as aware of him as he was of her. It was eating her up too.

Impossible. This was impossible.

He would not be good for this woman. And she would not be good for him. He had to drag his mind from thoughts of kissing her, of sweeping her up against him and making love to her where they stood, and back to…

Her son. Jesse.

She blinked and he realised he'd said Jesse's name out loud. 'You said something about the way I turned him down?' The words emerged on a growl, but he couldn't help it.

'Yes, the way you turned him down.' Her eyes took on the full ferocity of another glare. She opened her mouth but no sound came out, as if something in his face had stalled her. She frowned. 'You don't even remember, do you?'

He tried to think back. He remembered a blinding flash of panic, that was about all.

'You had this look of absolute horror on your face and you boomed out this big 'No!' If that's not designed to frighten a child, I don't know what will.'

She was right, he didn't remember. Jet lag wouldn't get him off the hook here.

'How would you have felt if I'd reacted like that when you asked me out for dinner?'

He remembered how he'd felt when she'd ordered him to cancel, and found his answer.

'It'd be unforgivable. Don't you think children deserve common courtesy?'

He was appalled at the picture she painted. Had he really been that abrupt? 'I am honestly sorry. I didn't mean to hurt Jesse's feelings or to frighten him. I…' He didn't know how to explain it. He didn't want to explain it. But he couldn't excuse his behaviour, not even to himself. 'I'll apologise to Jesse.' It was the least he could do.

'No, you won't. You'll stay away from my son. I don't want the likes of you confusing him, messing with his head. He's seven. He's just a little boy. He doesn't need that.'

And Simon knew she was right.

'All right.' He nodded though his head had never felt so heavy. 'I'm not trying to mess with anyone's head. I don't want to hurt anyone.'

But she'd turned away and he doubted she'd heard him.

She was right in that too, because what one meant to do and what one did weren't always the same thing.

Tour Three. A headache throbbed at Kate's temples and behind her eyes as she switched off the PA system, her commentary finally at an end. Simon's scent clogged up her senses and she wondered if this day would ever end.

She told herself she was glad Jesse was spending the next few days with his dad. It would get him out of the house and away from the God-awful tension between her and Simon. That kind of tension couldn't be good for anyone. She had a feeling she'd be a testament to that fact in a couple of days' time.

With Jesse at Paul's, it meant she didn't have to keep up a bright flow of chatter for Jesse's benefit. For a while there this morning she'd been in danger of flagging and that wouldn't do. It wouldn't do at all.

With Jesse at Paul's he wouldn't be subjected to any more of Simon's snubs.

She recalled the look of…of almost nausea that had crossed Simon's face when she'd taken him to task about that. It was as if he hadn't had any comprehension whatsoever of how his rejection might've hurt Jesse. And when he'd realised…

No, she wouldn't think about that. Her instincts about this man were all wrong. She refused to trust them. She steered *The Merry Dolphin* out into the middle of the bay, away from other boats, away from other obstacles.

The only problem with Jesse staying at Paul's? It left her and Simon in the house together. Alone. Without Jesse as a buffer.

Or a reminder.

She swallowed. She wouldn't panic. She just had to remember Simon was a lord who didn't like kids, and she was a single mum who did. She tried to fix his look of utter horror in her mind, the one that had slammed into place when she'd suggested he play cricket with Jesse, but it shifted, replaced by his look of nausea when he'd realized he'd hurt her son's feelings. An expression that told her she might have misjudged him.

An expression that lied.

She realised she was scowling and hastily pasted on another smile as she scanned the bay for any last sightings of dolphins. Ten more minutes and she could steer *The Merry Dolphin* back to the marina.

She glanced around at her passengers—holiday-makers enjoying the sun, the fresh air and the sense of freedom weekends brought. She tried to pull some of that into her psyche, but it didn't work. It didn't seem to be working for at least one of her passengers either. Mr Kennedy looked decidedly green around the gills.

She slowed *The Merry Dolphin*'s speed, adjusted the steering a fraction to smooth out the ride. She cast another glance at Mr Kennedy. She kept a close watch for signs of seasickness in her passengers. Normally. Today the bay was calm, and *The Merry Dolphin* was steady and sturdy but, as her father used to say, some people got seasick in the bath tub.

Mrs Kennedy stared merrily out at the view, oblivious to her husband's distress. Strain deepened the creases around Mr Kennedy's mouth and he turned a sickly shade of grey. She caught his gaze and pointed to the lined paper bags she kept on a shelf beneath the controls. He shook his head.

'We'll be back at the marina in under ten minutes,' she assured him. 'The breeze in your face might help.' She pointed towards the back of the boat to several spare seats. 'Some people swear by it.' Up here at the front, near the wheel and controls, Kate and the passengers closest were protected from the weather by a bank of Perspex windows.

He nodded and rose, and the last of the colour left his face. With a groan, he clutched his chest and pitched forward.

Kate abandoned the wheel to catch him and lower him to the deck as gently as she could—which wasn't very as he had to weigh at least two hundred pounds. Mrs Kennedy scrambled down beside Kate and started screaming her husband's name and shaking him. Kate grabbed the mouthpiece to the PA. 'Archie, I need you up here right now.' Then she dropped it, knocked the boat into neutral and turned back to Mr Kennedy.

A heart attack! He was having a heart attack!

Kate went cold all over. Her limbs and fingers grew heavy. No, no. She couldn't freeze. She forced herself to move. 'Keep back, please,' she ordered the concerned passengers who crowded around. 'Back to your seats.' She tried to inject authority into her voice and failed miserably. 'We need to give him air.'

Archie appeared, took in the situation and leapt straight to the wheel, pushing the boat back into motion. 'I'll call the ambulance.'

She nodded to let him know she'd heard. She checked Mr Kennedy's pulse. It was weak, but it was there. And he was still breathing. 'Please, everyone, back to your seats.' She almost sobbed the words as she felt the situation start to slip from her control.

Then, magically, Simon was there. And, with an ease she'd have applauded if she had the time, he had people back in their seats, giving her the room to roll Mr Kennedy into the recovery position.

Mrs Kennedy clawed at Kate's arm. 'What's wrong with him? Is he going to be all right? What are you doing?' With each question her voice rose.

And then Simon was there again, drawing Mrs Kennedy back onto the bench and holding her, soothing her, and it gave Kate enough time to brief the emergency service team on the phone about Mr Kennedy's symptoms. The information would be passed on to the paramedics who'd be waiting on the pier. She closed her eyes and prayed Mr Kennedy would hold on till then. She had a first aid certificate—every two years she attended a refresher course—but she'd never been called upon to use it. She'd hoped she never would be.

'Kate?'

Her eyes flew open. She couldn't hide her strain, her fear, from Simon's clear grey gaze. And at the moment she didn't care.

'Would it be okay if Joan held Rodney's hand?' he asked gently.

Mrs Kennedy—Joan—stared at Kate, her eyes full of fear but she was otherwise outwardly composed. How Simon had pulled off such a miracle in so short a time Kate had no idea, but she wanted to hug him.

She nodded mutely and shuffled down so Mrs Kennedy could take her place at Mr Kennedy's head and hold his hand. 'Can he hear me?' Mrs Kennedy touched Kate's arm, her eyes so full of pleading Kate knew she had to oust all worst case scenarios from her mind.

'I don't know,' she admitted. 'But the one time I fainted, I couldn't move a muscle, I couldn't open my eyes, but I could hear everything that went on around me.'

Simon said, 'Why don't you tell him that everything is going to be just fine. That there's an ambulance on standby at the pier and that you're going to be beside him every step of the way.'

Mrs Kennedy set about doing exactly that, scolding her husband gently, wiping the hair back from his forehead and re-assuring him. Kate wanted to hug Simon again. Over Mrs Kennedy's head, she met his gaze. For some reason, having him here made her panic recede.

'Kate? Is there anything else you need me to do? I do have a certificate in first aid.'

Her panic receded further. She mouthed 'heart attack', so he knew what they were dealing with. He nodded and she had a feeling he'd heard every word she'd spoken to the emergency personnel.

'Kate—' Archie's voice was terse '—we're nearly there and I'm going in fast.'

'Will you be okay here?' she asked Simon.

'Yes.'

His quiet confidence gave her the boost she needed. She leapt up to seize the dangling mouthpiece for the PA. 'Okay, folks, we've had a slight first aid emergency up here on the top deck. We'll be docking in a few moments with more speed than grace, I fear. I ask everyone to be seated and prepare for a bit of a bump. Please remain in your seats until the paramedics have boarded and then disembarked again with our casualty. Your co-operation in this will be greatly appreciated.'

Kate and Simon oversaw Mr and Mrs Kennedy to the ambulance. Before she leapt into the ambulance with her husband, Mrs Kennedy clasped Kate's face in her hands and kissed her cheek. 'Thank you. You moved so fast and knew precisely what to do. I can't thank you enough.' Then she disappeared.

Kate gulped in a breath before turning back to Simon. 'I want to thank you too. What you did...'

He shrugged. 'It was nothing more than crowd control.'

'It made all the difference.' As she said the words, she knew they were true. She and Simon had worked as a team. Efficient. Effective. She told herself it didn't change anything.

'You were the one who made the difference, Kate. You did everything you could, and you did it by the book.'

She had a feeling she wouldn't have managed that if he hadn't been there. His strength had bolstered her flagging confidence, had diminished her panic.

'But I'm glad I could help.' Then he turned and leapt back on board *The Merry Dolphin*.

After a moment's hesitation, Kate followed.

Tour Four. Kate's headache thumped into full-bodied life. She and Simon worked side by side behind the bar and some sixth sense she never knew she had tracked his every movement. He was all she could smell. They didn't talk much. Despite their jaw-grinding awareness of each other, that awful sense of awkwardness had gone. Kate had a feeling that might be the worst sign of all.

CHAPTER FIVE

KATE sensed the precise moment Simon entered the kitchen. She did her best to keep her back and shoulders relaxed. Her stomach tightened and clenched, but she figured he wouldn't notice that beneath the oversized T-shirt she wore.

'Coffee?' She tried to keep her voice if not bright then at least level. 'Or a beer?'

He'd earned both. He'd insisted on joining her on *The Merry Dolphin* again today. Like her, he'd worked a half day. Had said he wanted to pay his way in return for her hospitality.

Today he'd relaxed into it. Today he'd stopped shadowing her every move. Today he'd chatted and joked with the passengers as if born to the job.

Today she hadn't known which way was up.

He'd still avoided the children, though.

'A beer would be great. I'll get it,' he said when she made a move towards the fridge. 'You don't need to wait on me.'

She managed to feign a deep interest in her feet as he walked across the room. She couldn't prevent her eyes from flicking towards him once he was safely past her, though. Then he bent down to peer into the refrigerator's depths and...

Omigosh! She fanned her face. Nice butt.

'You want one?'

The lift of his lips, the cheek crease, told her he'd caught her ogling. Her throat closed over—previous experience told her the floor would not open up and swallow her. She shook her head and pointed to the coffee machine, which had just gurgled into life. Then did her best not to notice his fresh-from-the-shower crispness, the way damp darkened hair somehow highlighted the golden glow his skin had taken on after only two days in the sun. It was impossible, of course—Simon oozed health and vitality. She kept her eyes on the ceiling as he sauntered back across the room to lean one hip against the kitchen table.

The cool, clean scent of him invigorated her.

He hadn't glowered at the children today.

She stiffened from her slouch and did her best to shove that wayward thought right out of her head. Hope did not belong in any equation involving her and Simon. If she were honest, it never had. Even before the kid thing. He was here for two weeks. What on earth had she thought would happen between them in only two weeks?

She shook herself. 'I just got off the phone from Mrs Kennedy. Mr Kennedy is going to be just fine. They're treating his turn—as Mrs Kennedy calls it—as a warning.'

'She must be relieved.'

'Absolutely.' It was nearly impossible not to look at him, but she managed it. Just. 'She asked me to thank you again.'

'Not necessary.'

'That's what I said.'

Silence filled the spaces between them.

'Kate?'

He snapped open the top of his beer. She jumped. 'Hmm?'

'I didn't cancel our dinner date for this evening.'

It took a moment to drag her gaze from a mouth that uttered words in the kind of accent she'd love to sigh and stretch out under. Her pulse kicked up a notch when the import of his words sank through the hormone-befuddled haze that was currently her brain. She cast a deliberately casual glance at the clock on the kitchen wall—just after six.

'There's still time. You're welcome to use the phone in the hall.'

'Which gives you roughly an hour and a half to get ready,' he continued as if she hadn't spoken.

He took a swig of his beer, head tilted back, long tanned column of throat on display. Kate pushed away from the bench, seized the milk from the fridge and ordered herself not to look at him. 'I told you to cancel. I—'

'You want me to give up my one chance to eat at Fletchers?'

She sloshed milk all over the bench top. She abandoned the carton to spin and face him. 'Fletchers? You made a dinner reservation at Fletchers?' No, she couldn't have heard right. At this time of year, Fletchers was booked out months in advance.

'That's right, Fletchers. And now you're telling me you want me to cancel?'

She hadn't misheard. Fletchers!

Was he crazy? One didn't cancel a table at Fletchers.

She forced her body back against the bench, fought for common sense. Fought against the betraying thread of excitement that trickled through her whenever she glanced at him. All she got for her trouble was the cold stickiness against her back as spilt milk seeped into the cotton of her T-shirt.

'Ugh!' She reached back and pulled wet cotton off her skin but when Simon's eyes rested for the briefest moment on her front she let it drop with a squawk. Cold milk was exactly what she needed. She folded her arms over her chest. 'Yes.' She gave one hard nod. 'That's exactly what I'm saying. Cancel Fletchers.'

'You want me to miss out on eating there?' He glared at her as if she were mad. He had a point.

'Go alone.'

He raised an eyebrow, his lip curling slightly.

Fine. 'Take Felice when she gets back.'

'You think Fletchers will give me the time of day if I cancel now?'

Not a chance. She couldn't help herself. 'How on earth did you manage to get a table when you'd only been in Nelson's Bay for what…a matter of hours?'

'It wasn't easy.'

She snorted. 'From what I've heard, it's damn near impossible.'

'But when they found out I was the seventh Lord of Holm...'

Her jaw dropped. 'You're joking?'

'Nope.'

He grinned that low grin. The sexy one that brought cheek creases into serious play. The wet patch on her back turned warm and sticky. So did her insides.

'Outrageous, isn't it?'

'Totally.' Then she realised he meant Fletchers and how they'd pandered to his title. 'Absolutely.'

'And you seriously want me to cancel?'

Regret pitched through her, ousting the warmth, the trickling excitement. 'If you don't want to eat on your own, then yes. You and me, Simon, it isn't going to work. Going on a date is ridiculous.'

He shifted his weight to face her more fully, that cute butt of his resting on the pine surface of her kitchen table.

'Okay, so I agree it's not going to work.'

And she'd known she wouldn't get an argument about that. So why was it so hard to keep the corners of her mouth from drooping?

'It is pointless, you and me going on a date,' he continued. 'But when did you last eat out at Fletchers?'

Danny's twenty-first birthday.

'All I'm asking is that we go as friends, just for a nice meal. Which means it isn't really a date at all.'

Friends—her and Simon? 'Does that mean you'll let me pay for my half of the meal?'

'No.' He said the word gently, the grey of his eyes clear and kind, but resolute. 'This is a thank you for all of your hospitality.'

Behind her the coffee machine spluttered. Without turning, she reached behind and switched it off. She'd given up all thoughts of a caffeine kick. With Simon in the house she didn't need any more kicks. 'You've spent the last day and a half working aboard *The Merry Dolphin*. I suspect you won't let me pay you for it. I think that's thanks enough.'

'And I suspect that if you'd needed another crew member you'd have hired one. I was free to jump off whenever I wanted. I was having fun.' He paused. 'But if you won't let me thank you for allowing me the use of your guest room, then I think that's an indication you might prefer it if I arranged alternative accommodation.'

'No!' The word shot out of her before she could stop it. He was Felice's brother. Danny's brother-in-law. It was only right that he stay here. She remembered how much he'd helped her with the Kennedys yesterday. 'Friends?' She tested the word.

His gaze never left hers. 'Can you be friends with a man who isn't into children, but who'll promise from hereon to treat Jesse with the same consideration as he treats you?'

'Yes.' That was easy. She didn't even have to think about it. Some people didn't want children. She didn't have a problem with that. Different strokes and whatnot. Some people shouldn't have children and perhaps Simon was one of them. Problem was, she could never become involved with someone like that.

'So you'll come to Fletchers with me?'

'Yes.'

He smiled again—cheek creases and all—and she couldn't help smiling back. Their eyes locked, he kept smiling and she kept smiling. Oh, good Lord. Distraction. She needed a distraction.

'What time did you make the reservation?'

'Seven-thirty.'

'What?' She jerked to attention with a yelp.

'Is that a problem?'

She did her best impression of a haughty socialite. 'I'll have you know that most women need at least three hours of primping and preening before stepping into the hallowed foyer of Fletchers.'

He took a sip of his beer before looking her up and down. Kate's blood did a silly little jig in her veins. The fingers that gripped his beer were long and lean. He had nice hands and a great grin. And eyes to die for—smoky, smouldering eyes outlined in dark, dark lashes and they were looking at her as if those long, lean fingers of his and those firm, tilted-at-the-corner lips would prefer to be holding her, touching her, than they would that can of beer. Which was a crazy thought because they were just friends. Nothing more.

He set the can down on the table. 'You could go as you are and still be the most stunning woman in the room.'

For a moment Kate could've sworn the actual air between them sizzled with heat shimmer. She blinked and it subsided. 'Now you're just being extravagant,' she said, trying to throw off the compliment, but her voice wobbled. She pointed towards the door. 'I'll…um…go and get ready.' And she fled.

An hour later, Kate stepped into the living room but whatever she'd meant to say got lost somewhere between brain and mouth when her eyes landed on Simon.

She swallowed. She reminded herself that dribbling down her front was a seriously bad look. He wore a black dinner jacket and bow-tie, which contrasted crisply with a fresh white dress shirt, and he looked debonair and sophisticated and to-die-for. Hero material for some movie set. But it was the way he stared at her that had her words melting on her tongue. She had a feeling his smoky gaze could spark a fire that could consume them both. She must have been crazy to agree to this.

He cleared his throat and motioned to her. 'I can't believe, even given three hours of primping and preening, that you could look better than you do now.' A smile curved his lips; appreciation lit his eyes. 'Kate, you are beautiful.'

The simple sincerity of his compliment had the heat blossoming in her cheeks and pleasure tumbling through her. 'Thank you. You don't look too shabby yourself.' Maniacal laughter rang through her head at the understatement.

She wore her favourite dress—a silver sheath the quick-silver colour of the bay at midnight on a full moon. It shimmered as she moved and was fitted to the knee, where it then flared out to swirl around her calves. She'd teamed it with a pair of high-heeled silver sandals, a beaded wrap and a tiny clutch. He kept staring and the heat kept building inside her.

'Should we walk?' She pasted on a smile. Fletchers was on the boardwalk above the marina.

Simon glanced down at her shoes and one corner of his mouth lifted. 'They look more like dancing shoes, Kate. Not walking shoes.'

'I could change them for my trainers, but they might spoil the effect.'

'I'll drive.'

The heat dissipated a little. Relief pounded through her in equal measure with regret. Gritting her teeth, she did her best to ignore the regret. She did not need the strain or temptation of a fifteen-minute walk home in the moonlight with Simon. He'd take her arm because he was that kind of man—thoughtful, heedful of the niceties—and his scent would drench her senses. She'd lean into him to test his strength and balance; she wouldn't be able to help herself. They'd stop, turn to each other in the moonlight and…

No! No! No!

Taking the car was far more sensible. She bit back a sigh and led the way through the house and outside to the car.

Kate couldn't remember the last time she'd enjoyed a meal more. The food was heavenly, of course. This *was* Fletchers, after all. The prawns were moist, the poached salmon succulent, the lemon-myrtle tart refreshing, the champagne French and the view to-die-for. They sat in an intimate alcove at a table for two—all candlelit white linen and crystal—with the fairy tale lights of the bay spread out before them. As a setting, it was perfect.

As a dinner companion, so was Simon.

He went out of his way to make her laugh and relax—paying her compliments so extravagant that nobody in their right mind could take them seriously. And somehow that seemed to shrink the attraction between them to a manageable level. Everything became easy and free between them again. Like it had at the beach on Friday.

Only this time there was no self-deception.

And, because things were so easy and relaxed, when Simon suggested a walk along the boardwalk after dinner, she readily agreed. 'I need to after stuffing myself silly with all of that divine food,' she confessed.

He glanced down at her shoes and his mouth kinked upwards. 'We'll make it a short walk.'

She smiled because he was right. These shoes were killers. He might do his best to hide it, or maybe she'd done her best not to see it, but he had an innate sense of protectiveness several kilometres wide. And it warmed her.

They walked along in silence for a bit, the only sound the swishing of the tiny waves as they curled up onto the sand and back again. The kind of sound that Kate thought could lull a person into a false sense of security…if they let it.

Finally, she stopped. If they went much further they'd be right above the spot where they'd kissed. She didn't want Simon recognising it…remembering it. She did her best to eradicate her own recollections.

She spread her arms out in a futile attempt to embrace the view and distract him. 'Heavenly, isn't it?'

'Yes.'

But his eyes were on her face and not on the view. He already had recognised their location. She could tell from the way his eyes travelled over the park, the beach, and the flare in their depths told her he remembered that kiss.

Heaven help her but her womb tugged and throbbed in instant response.

'I've had a wonderful night, Simon.' She swallowed. She wanted to tell him not to spoil it now, but the words wouldn't come.

'I have too.'

He reached out, pushed a strand of hair back behind her ear. His touch lingered on her cheek and it took all of her strength not to lean into it.

'There was something I didn't tell you down there in the park on Friday.'

She shouldn't ask. Instinct warned her not to ask. 'Oh?'

'That wasn't just about the best kiss I'd ever experienced. It was far and away the best. What's that saying—the best by a baker's dozen or something?'

'A country mile,' she murmured automatically. She had a feeling he'd got it deliberately wrong to make her laugh and she really wished she could. 'The best by a country mile.' But a girl needed air in her lungs to laugh. 'Simon, you have to forget about that kiss.' So did she.

He shook his head. 'I mean to cherish it.'

The admission stole her breath. When he turned to her in the moonlight, cupped her face with one hand, she didn't back away. When his mouth descended towards hers, she didn't ask him to stop. When his lips brushed hers, she couldn't contain a sigh. She didn't know who then took the step forward to close the gap between them—she felt so attuned to this man she thought it might have been both of them. Together. At the same time.

His head dipped again. His mouth covered hers, moved over her lips with a firmness, a sureness, that left her trembling. The kiss told her he knew her, that he liked her and wanted her. She opened up to him immediately and told him she knew him and liked him too.

Sensation and desire surged to life. His hands explored the curves of her hips and waist, touching off sparks and fireworks, urging her closer. Their moans and gasps mingled. His mouth on her throat…her hands working their way under his dress shirt to the bare skin of his back and stomach. The only sounds their sighs and the swishing of waves and the plashing of a night bird as it hit the water.

A night bird.

Water.

Kate didn't want to think, but one part of her mind kept niggling and niggling at her until she kinked open one eye…and saw stars, heard a car roar off down the street.

They were in a public place!

She took a step back. Simon released her immediately, then swore at whatever he saw in her face. She took in his kissed-to-within-an-inch-of-his-life dishevelment. And then her own. She took another step back and did what she could to straighten her dress, her hair…her mind.

'Simon, I don't do flings.' Even if her blood was doing a heck of a good impression of a Highland fling right now. 'You're only here for a fortnight. I have a child, so even if you do long-term commitment it won't be with me.' Her blood started to slow. 'This can't happen. I thought we'd agreed on that this afternoon.' She sagged as the last of her energy fizzed out of her.

Simon bent at the waist, rested his hands on his knees. Finally he straightened. 'You're right. I'm sorry.'

Kate took one look at the grim set of his lips and staggered across to a park bench, unsure if her legs would hold her up much longer. After a hesitation, Simon joined her.

'Don't even think of asking me if I'm okay,' she snapped when he opened his mouth. He closed it again. 'Of course I'm okay.' It was only a kiss. Even if it had felt more like a full-frontal assault on her senses.

He dragged a hand down his face, massaging the skin around his eyes, and she knew he hadn't emerged unscathed either. She forced her eyes to the front, stared out into the inky depths of the bay.

'Why don't you like children, Simon?'

She needed talk, chatter, to distance herself from the devastation of that kiss. It made her blurt out the question uppermost in her mind.

'It's not that I don't like them!' He reared back to stare at her. 'It's just that I'm no good with them.'

She blinked. She shook herself. 'What makes you think you're not good with them?'

He folded his arms and glared out at the water. 'Some people are good at business or sport. Others have musical talent or are good with children. I'm good at business. I'm okay at sport. I missed out on the good-with-children gene.'

Something inside her clicked. His disquiet when Jesse and Nick had camped in the back garden. His concern that riding the boom nets on *The Merry Dolphin* could be dangerous... She tried for light. She had to keep this light. 'And the musical talent?'

Obligingly his lips curved upwards, but it was more a polite attempt at a smile than the real thing. 'Zilch.'

The beach in front of them glittered white. On the water, a path to the moon, sprinkled with stars, shivered silver.

'I'm good at gardening. I'm great at piloting a nineteen point eight metre mono-hull with twin screws, and I'm good with kids. But I had to learn all of those things, Simon. I wasn't born with an innate talent for them.'

'You must've had a leaning towards them.'

'Nope, it was just fate or...or circumstances.'

He turned to meet her gaze and she shrugged. 'My father took me out on boats from the time I was a baby. I had a boat licence long before I ever had a car licence. Taking over Merry Dolphin Tours was a natural progression. It made my dad happy, and that was important to me.' She stared out at the water and bit back a sigh. 'The gardening was my mother's thing. My mother left home when I was six and Danny was just a baby.'

Simon took her hand. She squeezed it gratefully. Her mother's desertion still hurt all these years later.

'She loved the garden. When she left I decided to keep it up just in case she ever came back. She never did, but by the time

I'd come to that realisation…and come to terms with it…the gardening had become a habit. Somewhere along the way, I'd come to love it. And kids.' She started to laugh. 'Seriously, Simon, before Jesse I knew nothing about kids.'

He stared down into her laughing face, frown lines marring the perfection of his forehead. 'But you love him. And you've obviously done a great job of raising him.'

'Thank you. And yes, of course I love him, but I had to learn mothering as I went along. It's not something that just comes naturally, you know.'

Simon released her hand to stare moodily out to sea. Kate willed him to look at her. 'I don't believe there's any such thing as a good-with-children gene, Simon.'

His lips twisted. He laughed but it lacked mirth. 'You can't make me good with kids just by wishing it, Kate.'

She stared at him some more, taking in the stern lines of his mouth and the set of his shoulders. 'Someone or something has put you off children.'

He sent her an exasperated glare, resting his elbows on his knees. 'You don't give up, do you? Take my word for it. All my life I've been bad with children.'

Who had put that idea into his head?

Her heart started to thump. The expression on his face—proud, defensive, shuttered—made her want to cry. 'Fine,' she snapped back, because she wasn't going to cry. She might not be able to stop herself from caring, but she wouldn't cry. 'Give me one example of when you've been bad with children.'

The glare became a scowl. 'You're worse than Felice when it comes to nagging.'

In answer she folded her arms and raised an eyebrow.

'God give me strength,' he muttered under his breath. 'Fine! Last month I became godfather to a baby girl. She's my friend Tim's first.'

Kate unfolded her arms to stab a finger at him. 'There's at least one person who thinks you're okay with kids.'

'Give me a break, Kate. Where I come from, having a lord as a godfather is a status symbol.'

She hunched her shoulders at his bitterness. 'I think you're undervaluing yourself. I bet your friend Tim doesn't care if you're a lord or not.'

He didn't reply. She made herself unhunch. 'I don't see any proof yet.'

He stood, started to pace. 'During the christening service there's a point where I had to hold the baby.'

'Uh-huh.'

'Well…' He stopped pacing, shoving his hands in his trouser pockets. 'I couldn't.'

'What do you mean you couldn't?'

'Fiona, Tim's wife, kept telling me I was holding the baby all wrong. I tried to follow her instructions, but the baby kept squirming and there was this crazy long dress getting scrunched up and…'

'And…' Kate prompted. Good Lord. He hadn't dropped the baby in the font or anything, had he?

'It was a bloody nightmare! Fiona started yelling that I was going to drop the baby and snatched her up. There were all these other children running around and banging into things and breaking them. I've never been happier to get out of a place.'

Kate wanted to laugh but the expression on his face stopped her. She leapt up and moved across until she stood directly in front of him, her heart aching for him. 'Simon, all first-time mothers are paranoid and over-protective. You can't take something like that to heart. One does not automatically know how to hold a baby. It takes practice. You didn't hit a six the first ball you ever faced in cricket, did you?'

'No, but—'

'This is the same. Babies are really hard, especially when they're not your own.' She rolled her eyes. 'Especially when they're that small. Just because you were part of the christening from hell doesn't prove anything.'

'This is not an isolated incident, Kate, just the last in a long line.'

His hands went to his hips. Nice hips, she couldn't help noticing. She dragged her gaze back up to his face.

'None of my friends bring their children when they visit me.'

'I'm betting your house isn't child-friendly.' If he lived in some grand manor house it probably contained an array of antique vases and heirlooms that would make the mothers of toddlers break out into a cold sweat.

'I don't even know what child-friendly means,' he said, almost in triumph, as if this proved his point.

Did he really believe this nonsense? Had he ever considered the fact that his friends quite obviously sensed his discomfort when children were about and did what they could to put him at his ease?

'Simon—'

'A child was injured in my care once, Kate. I will not let that happen again.'

She glanced up into the lean, proud face—now shuttered—and a sheen of ice filmed her skin. She didn't try to offer him any kind of sympathy or condolence. She sensed he wouldn't welcome it. She took his arm and set his feet on the concrete path instead.

They walked along in silence for a while. 'Will you tell me about it?' she asked, ignoring the bite of her shoes. Something far more important than feet was at stake here.

'I was fourteen,' he finally said. He stopped. She didn't urge him forward. 'There'd been some do on at the estate the previous day, which was unusual because it was summer. My parents spent most summers abroad.

'Did you and Felice go abroad with them?'

'No.'

He didn't add anything further. Kate moistened her lips. Who had looked after them? One glance into his face and she thought it might be better not to ask. 'I'm sorry. There was this party…?'

'A few distant cousins on my mother's side stayed overnight

and it fell to me to keep the associated children out of the adults' hair the next day.'

'Why you?' She couldn't stop the question from popping out. 'I mean, didn't you have a nanny or something?'

Just for a moment, amusement lit his eyes. 'I was a fourteen-year-old boy, Kate.'

'Oh, right.' Of course! 'Fourteen-year-old boys don't need nannies.'

'"Bingo", to quote you.'

'Felice would have only been four. She must've had a nanny.'

Simon frowned. 'I can't place her nanny there that day at all.' He shrugged as if it didn't matter 'When I was at the estate, Felice would follow me around like a little shadow anyway. If her nanny was there she'd have rightly figured Felice was with me.'

And he hadn't minded? The fourteen-year-old boys she knew would chafe at the kind of restriction that would place on their freedom.

No, she could tell from his face that he hadn't minded. With their parents gone most summers, he'd have been Felice's only family, her only security.

And now Felice had run away.

Kate pressed a hand to her chest. The more she got to know this man, the more she could feel his pain...and his sense of failure.

'Where were you the rest of the time?'

He gazed at her blankly.

'You said Felice followed you around *when* you were at the estate.'

He stared straight ahead. 'Boarding school.'

Boarding school! 'Charming!' The word shot out of her. She covered her mouth with her hand. 'Sorry, I didn't mean—'

Amusement lit his eyes again as he turned to meet her gaze. 'So no boarding school for Jesse, then?'

'No way, José! I'm not going to miss out on watching him

grow up, on seeing him every day that I can. I mean, what's the point in having kids if…'

She broke off, cleared her throat, realising this was Simon's parents she was denigrating and perhaps that was not the most tactful move she'd made all night. 'And Felice?'

'Boarding school from the age of six. Like me.' He must've seen the look on her face because he added, 'My dear, boarding school is *de rigueur* in my circle.'

'I'd be setting a new trend,' she snapped back.

He threw his head back and laughed. 'I bet you would too but, according to my parents, boarding school was supposed to teach us backbone and duty. Independence.'

She folded her arms and tapped a foot. She had to leave off tapping when the straps of her shoes bit into her toes. 'I'd never leave something so important to a school.'

'No, I don't believe you would. You're a wonderful mother, Kate.'

He smiled down at her with such warmth she didn't know what to do. 'Thank you,' she gulped.

Had his mother been wonderful too?

She'd sent her children to boarding school. She'd spent the summer holidays abroad while her children stayed at the Holm estate. Kate didn't like the pictures her mind conjured.

'Kate?'

She snapped back to the present, tried to school her features. 'We're getting off the track.' She sent him a tight smile. 'All my fault, I'm afraid. You were telling me about the day after the party and finding yourself in charge of all those children. How many and how old?' she shot at him, taking his arm and urging him forward again.

'Not counting Felice, there were five of them.' He shrugged. 'I guess they ranged in age from six to eleven.'

So altogether he'd been in charge of six children between the ages of four and eleven? A fourteen-year-old boy? What on earth had these people been thinking? 'Young, then,' she managed.

'And loud.'

There was a sigh behind the words. She understood it too. Hung-over parents and rowdy children? Not a good mix.

He turned to her. 'What would you do to keep a bunch of noisy kids occupied?'

'If the weather's good?'

He nodded.

'A game of cricket on the beach.'

'Precisely.'

She let go of his arm and stared at him. Her stomach rolled over and over. 'You took them all to…I don't know, behind the stables, where they could make as much noise as they wanted and you started a game of cricket.'

'That's right.'

She'd asked him to play cricket with Jesse. On the beach. On his own. Had there been a pond? Had someone drowned? 'What happened?'

'Not the stables, but the machinery shed. A tractor had been left out overnight and a couple of the younger boys became most interested in it.'

She'd bet. Had he taken them for a ride—an over-confident fourteen-year-old—and had someone fallen off…or worse?

'But I eventually managed to shoo them away and we started playing.'

So far, so good.

'But someone got a ball in the face—bloody nose.'

She wrinkled her own nose in sympathy. 'It does happen, you know.' He couldn't blame himself for that.

'While I was dealing with that, a couple of the younger boys sneaked back to the tractor.'

Kate closed her eyes. When she opened them she realised he'd started walking again. She caught up with him.

'One climbed up onto it, somehow knocked it out of gear, fell off when it started moving.' He dragged a hand down his face. 'The back wheel ran over his leg, crushing his ankle.'

Kate pulled him to a halt because her heart had started to burn more than her feet. 'Simon, that was an accident.'

'An avoidable one.'

'It was *not* your fault.' There should've been adults around. A fourteen-year-old should not have been made to feel responsible for that!

'My parents certainly held me responsible.' The anguish in his eyes was quickly masked. 'They were appalled at my negligence.'

'Your… No! They should've been appalled at their own.' She stared into his closed and shuttered face. 'No,' she whispered. 'They were wrong. Simon, I swear to you, they were wrong.'

But she could tell he didn't believe her. 'Children are so quick. When Jesse was five we were playing in the back garden. I went inside to get us some drinks—I wouldn't have been gone forty seconds. In that time Jesse had climbed a tree, which he knew he wasn't allowed to do. He fell out of it and broke his arm.'

'Nobody would ever accuse you of negligence, Kate.'

'But can't you see it's the same—Jesse's accident and your cousin's accident?'

'No, it's not.' He rested his hands on his knees as if the weight pressing down on him had become too much. 'Lewis walks with a limp to this very day. He gets about with a cane.'

Her heart filled with sympathy for this bear of a man who only wanted to keep people safe. Jesse's accident had shaken her confidence, had filled her with nameless fears for a while. And if Paul had started throwing around accusations…but he hadn't. Everyone had been supportive.

Simon hadn't had that kind of support and reassurance!

Her hands bunched into fists. 'What happened to you afterwards, Simon?'

He straightened. 'I was sent to military boarding school.'

She didn't know what that meant, but it sounded grim.

'Lots of marching,' he explained. He smiled, but it didn't reach his eyes. 'Apparently it's character building.'

Fiddlesticks!

'I was sent there the next day.'

And then it hit her. They'd sent him away from Felice. They'd drummed into him that he couldn't be trusted around small children and then they'd sent him away from Felice. Nausea rose up through her. His parents had deserved to be skinned alive.

Simon suddenly swung round to her. He gripped her shoulders, his eyes burning down into hers. 'You have to see why it's better that I stay away from children.'

No, she didn't!

'Me and children, we don't mix.'

'Simon, you—'

'No!'

He cupped her face, pressing his thumbs to her lips to stem the flow of her words. The determination in his eyes shredded her heart. 'I'm not cut out for it, Kate. I…I just can't do it.'

Very gently he removed his hands. The mask she'd started to recognise slipped back into place. He set his shoulders and lifted his chin. 'I have no intention of becoming a father.'

The words rang a death knell through a last hope she hadn't even known she'd clutched near.

CHAPTER SIX

ON WEDNESDAY afternoon, when Simon arrived back at Kate's after a day of sightseeing, he followed the sound of shouts and laughter out to the back garden. Since Sunday night, he and Kate had skirted around each other—polite and civilised, doing their best to keep their distance, doing what they could to make things easy for themselves.

During the day, Kate had gone to work. During the day, Simon had explored beaches, inlets and bays, had gone swimming and snorkelling. In short, he was having a holiday. Like Kate had told him to.

And it had helped.

He didn't want to admit it, but it had. Tension he'd grown so used to that he'd forgotten it even existed had eased out of him, leaving him feeling more relaxed than he had in years. It didn't stop him from clenching from the inside out whenever he saw Kate, though. Like he was doing right now.

Kate stood between a makeshift goal consisting of a wheelie bin on one side and Jesse's bike on the other. 'C'mon.' She half crouched, gesturing with both hands. 'Give it your best shot.'

Jesse stood several feet away, a soccer ball at his feet. Kate had told Simon that Jesse would be back from his dad's today.

Or was that warned?

Jesse screwed his face up in concentration. So did Kate. For a moment they looked so alike it made Simon grin.

Jesse took one step back, then another. He pulled in a breath, then he surged forward and kicked the ball. It bounced off the garage wall behind Kate. Jesse raced around the garden, arms above his head. 'That's another one to me.'

'Odds are stacked in your favour, bucko!' She bounced on the balls of her feet, pretended to spit on her hands. 'I was off balance. C'mon—again.'

Simon wasn't sure who was having more fun, Kate or Jesse. He laughed out loud at her comical excitement when she saved the next shot.

She swung to him and a smile lit her face. 'Hey, Simon, have a good day?'

'I did.' He lowered himself onto one of the chairs around the outdoor table, content to watch. Jesse kicked another goal and Simon remembered his manners. 'Hello, Jesse.'

It earned him a grin. 'G'day.' Jesse drawled the word out as long as he could. 'My dad said that's what I had to say to you when I saw you next 'cause it's real Ocker.'

Simon blinked. 'Ocker?'

'You know, Australian.' Jesse drawled that out long and hard too. 'He said it'd make you laugh.'

Simon made himself laugh and Jesse turned back to his game, apparently satisfied.

'What did you get up to today?' Kate asked as Jesse put another goal past her.

Apparently she could play with Jesse and talk to him at the same time. He couldn't manage to look at her and talk at the same time. She wore short shorts and the long length of her tanned legs had his tongue cleaving to the roof of his mouth. He dragged his gaze to Jesse, setting up for his next shot, instead. 'I discovered Fingal Bay today.'

'Ooh, it's beautiful, isn't it?'

Another goal to Jesse. Following the ball's progress, though, brought Kate squarely back into Simon's line of sight. 'Er...yeah.'

'Was it low tide? Did you walk out on the spit to Fingal Island?'

'I did.' He kept his gaze solidly on a colourful bird in a nearby flame tree—a rainbow lorikeet. Kate had identified it for him earlier in the week.

'And did you see dolphins?'

Her simple love for the dolphins touched him. 'Yes, and I think they're amazing.' But not as amazing as her.

'They run these fabulous sunset kayak tours around there. The dolphins nearly always come and swim with the kayaks. It's so still and quiet and magical.'

He had a feeling that a sunset anywhere in the world with Kate would be magical. An ache gripped him. 'Perhaps we should do that some time.' He glanced at Jesse. 'All of us,' he added. Jesse might prove a convenient buffer. 'When Felice gets back.'

'Cool,' Jesse said.

'Cool,' Kate said.

Her smile made him feel a million dollars.

Jesse kept practising his goal kicks, Kate kept trying to save them and their chatter died out. Finally Kate called out, 'Uncle! Sorry, Jesse, but I'm knackered.'

She collapsed at the table with Simon and sent him a grin. He grinned back, but concern shot through him. She looked tired. Lines of strain had appeared around her eyes and mouth. She looked as if she hadn't slept in a week.

Because of him?

Guilt and regret stole through him. 'You look exhausted, Kate. Why don't you go and lie back in a hot bath?' Felice had always extolled the benefits of a hot bath and if there was ever a candidate in need of one now, it was Kate.

'Ooh, that sounds divine.' He could see her practically salivate. But then her gaze darted to Jesse.

Simon shifted uncomfortably on his chair. He didn't want to be left alone with the boy, but... He glanced back at Kate and found her watching him uncertainly and with the teensiest bit of hope flaring to life in her big blue eyes. Then the hope died.

Simon shoved his shoulders back. 'You're only going to be in there, aren't you?' He hitched his head towards the house. 'Within earshot.' She'd only be a shout away. And she deserved some down time.

If she was concerned about Jesse, that was one thing.

But if she was concerned about him…

'You could tell him not to leave the garden and not to climb trees and not to play with knives and stuff, couldn't you?'

'Yes, but…' She shook herself. 'I have to get the dinner on.'

'I'll do that.'

The blue eyes flashed with hope again. 'Are you serious?'

'Utterly. Take an hour out for yourself.' She obviously needed it.

'Okay.' She pursed her lips, before biting the lower one. 'Jesse will be fine. He knows what he is and isn't allowed to do, and he's a good kid.'

Simon nodded, relieved that not too much was expected of him on the Jesse front.

'And I was just going to heat up a quiche for dinner and throw some veggies on to steam.'

His relief fled, but he refused to let that show. 'No problem.'

'Simon, you're a doll.' She leaned across as if to kiss his cheek, but pulled back in double-quick time. 'Um…thank you.'

'Take your time,' he called out as she tripped into the house. Then he turned to Jesse, who'd followed the conversation with apparent interest.

'Will you go in goal for me?' Hopeful blue eyes so like Kate's lifted to Simon's. 'It's just…I can't kick the ball as hard as I want at Mum 'cause she's a girl.'

Simon choked back a laugh. Then, 'All right,' he agreed slowly. He couldn't see any harm in that. He remembered going in goal for Felice more times than he could count when she'd gone through her soccer phase.

Jesse grinned a grin like Kate's.

'But I'd better warn you, I'm a better goalie than your mum.'

He'd barely got into position, though, when the ball went whizzing past him. 'Hey! I wasn't ready.'

Jesse's grin filled with mischief. 'How much time do you want?'

'Brat!' He crouched in readiness and tried not to grin.

The game was hard and fast. Simon couldn't keep from praising Jesse's finer efforts—the kid really had a great kick on him. Jesse scored more goals than Simon saved, but Simon saved more goals than Kate had.

'Yes!' Jesse did a victory dance. 'That's fifteen to me and only six to you.'

'Hey, the odds are stacked in your favour, bucko.' He borrowed the term from Kate. 'Now, if I was kicking and you were in goal…'

'All right, then,' Jesse offered generously. 'We'll swap.'

Simon stiffened. What if he kicked the ball into Jesse's face? What if he kicked it too hard and Jesse sprained a wrist trying to save it? What if…? 'I…er…can't.'

'Why not?'

'I told your mum I'd get dinner ready.'

'Can you cook?'

'Um, no.' But how hard could it be to warm up a quiche and prepare a few vegetables?

Jesse groaned. 'And I'm really hungry!'

Simon's stomach rumbled in sympathy. Jesse's eyes widened when he heard it. 'Dinner's ages away yet, isn't it?'

Yep, it probably was.

'You know what I sometimes eat when I get home from school?'

'What?'

'Come and see.'

Simon followed Jesse into the house and watched as he grabbed two bowls and two spoons and set them on the table. He collected a box of breakfast cereal and a carton of milk, then sat. He stared at Simon expectantly.

Obviously he expected Simon to join him. Simon sat too. 'Are you allowed to snack between meals?'

Jesse rolled his eyes before fixing Simon with a withering glare.

'Sorry.' Simon held up both hands. 'I don't know about these things.' He wasn't sure that he liked the sudden gleam that lit Jesse's eyes.

Jesse filled both bowls with cereal and milk. He pushed one towards Simon. 'It's really good.'

Simon hesitated, but it was clear that Jesse expected him to eat it. He grimaced after his first mouthful. 'Hell, Jesse, this is awfully sweet.' He wondered if he was allowed to say *hell* around a seven-year-old.

Jesse nodded happily. 'The best thing is the chocolate comes off the cereal and turns it all to chocolate milk.'

And that was supposed to be a good thing?

'You'd better hurry up and eat it,' Jesse added. ''Cause if Mum catches us we're in big trouble.'

Simon nearly dropped his spoon. 'You said—'

'Tricked ya!'

Jesse grinned, so pleased with himself that it took all of Simon's strength to hold back a laugh.

'And you'll get into more trouble than me, 'cause I'll say you told me it was okay and you're the adult.'

'Brat.' Simon pointed his spoon at Jesse. 'You'll keep, but in the meantime shut up and eat. I want this mess cleared up before your mother sees it.'

* * *

Kate lay back in the bath tub and heaved a sigh of pure pleasure at the enveloping warmth of hot water against her skin, against muscles that ached for no good reason. She heard the clink of spoons scraping china bowls and grinned.

She'd recognised the thump of the soccer ball against the garage wall before. Somehow, Jesse had enticed Simon to play. And now, unless she was very much mistaken, they were both eating bowls of cereal—Jesse was obviously getting it all his own way. She cocked her head to one side and listened. Yep, definitely two spoons at play there.

All Simon needed was a push in the right direction and he'd soon see what was plain to her—that he'd make a great father, that shutting himself off from the joys and pleasures of fatherhood was not the answer. Oh, she knew he'd return to England at the end of this fortnight and no amount of heart-racing and palm-sweating and toe-curling on her behalf would change that.

She had to try and stop all that heart-racing and palm-sweating and toe-curling. It complicated everything. It couldn't be good for her health.

A burst of laughter broke into her thoughts. She smiled and stretched, plugged the spout of the tap with her big toe. Dinner would be late tonight, but she didn't care, not one little bit. She'd stay here for a bit longer and let Jesse work his magic.

She'd try and work some of her own later this evening, and hopefully, when he left Australia, Simon would be happier than when he'd arrived.

Once Kate had Jesse settled in bed, she pulled a bottle of Chardonnay from the fridge, two wineglasses from the cupboard and slipped back outside. They'd eaten dinner at the outdoor table—it had fitted the holiday mood of the afternoon—and she didn't want that mood dissipating yet. Simon looked relaxed and healthy…and heart-stoppingly heavenly. In another month his hair would be the perfect length.

But he wouldn't be here for another month.

'Wine?' she squeaked.

Simon's cheek creases appeared in all their heart-popping glory. No heart-popping, she ordered.

He took the wine and the corkscrew, opened the bottle and filled their glasses. She couldn't help but return his smile. 'I guess that's a yes, then.'

'Did Jesse settle down all right?'

'He was asleep before his head hit the pillow. I don't know what the two of you got up to while I was in the bath but he certainly enjoyed it.'

Simon's wineglass halted halfway to his mouth. A lovely, lovely mouth, she couldn't help noticing. 'Why? What did he say?'

'Nothing.' She suppressed a grin. 'Why?'

'No reason,' he mumbled. He took a sip and brightened. 'He's a great kid.'

'I think so,' she agreed.

'Tell me about your decision to have him. I'm guessing it wasn't exactly a planned pregnancy?'

'No, it wasn't.' She grimaced, then tried to smile. 'Paul and I had only just started dating when my father died unexpectedly of a heart attack.'

'I'm sorry.' He reached a hand towards her, but he didn't touch her. 'It must've been hard losing him suddenly like that.'

'It was. All of a sudden it felt as if I no longer had an anchor in the world.' She paused, remembering the sheer awfulness of that time. 'I turned to Paul for comfort.'

'And Jesse was the result?'

'And Jesse was the result,' she agreed. She smiled, this time without any effort. 'I haven't regretted my decision for a single moment.'

'And Paul?'

'He was understandably shell-shocked at the time, of course, and we stopped dating by mutual consent before Jesse was born.' Her lips twisted into a rueful smile. 'We never did have the kind of romance that set the world on fire, but he's always been supportive. He's a great dad to Jesse and a good friend to me.'

'I'm glad.'

And she believed him.

Although the sun had sunk behind the horizon some time ago, the warmth of the day still lingered in the air. Simon set his glass down and stretched with a groan. Kate laughed. 'Sore, huh?'

'I haven't played goalie since Felice was about thirteen and soccer mad.'

She shot forward in her seat, the wine in her glass sloshing over the sides. 'So you did play with her?'

One side of his oh-so-kissable mouth lifted. 'I had to. In the interests of peace and quiet and sanity. If nagging were an Olympic sport, Felice would take out gold.'

Relief rushed through her. Despite all his parents had done, he'd maintained a relationship with Felice. It made her feel happier than it had any right to. 'You were her big brother. She looked up to you.'

His smile dipped 'I guess she did. Once upon a time.' He shrugged. 'She was just a bored little girl and there was no one else around to pester.'

He must've been off at university or working by this time. And yet she'd bet he'd spared Felice as much time as he could've.

'You know what, Simon? I don't think I'd have liked your parents very much.' She glared at the deeper shadows of her garden, then added a hurried, 'No offence meant.' Good Lord! Did she always have to blurt out what she was thinking as soon as she thought it?

'None taken.'

'What I meant is, I believe we'd have disagreed about the way to bring up children.'

'I believe you're right.' His smile broadened. 'Your parenting strategies are certainly vastly different.'

'Parenting strategies,' she snorted. 'You mean they had one?'

'Absolutely. They saw it as their beholden duty to provide an heir and a spare. And to provide for said heir and spare's material needs. In many ways our upbringing was very privileged.'

Privileged? Ha! 'Heaven forbid they spend any quality time with you,' she muttered. She glanced across at him. Tension hadn't shot back into his shoulders, but she sensed he wasn't as relaxed as he appeared. 'You must've been dreadfully lonely as a little boy rattling around in that big house on your own.'

'There were an ample number of household staff to keep me company.'

She thought of Jesse abandoned like that…and then imagined a younger version of Simon. The picture she painted almost broke her heart.

Simon glanced at her, then rolled his eyes at whatever he saw reflected in her face. 'Seriously, Kate, the solitude never bothered me.'

'And Felice, did it bother her?'

He was silent for a moment. 'Yes,' he finally said. 'It bothered her.'

Of course it had! 'I can barely begin to imagine the support and comfort you were to her,' she stated gently.

He shifted on his seat, lifting the wine bottle as if meaning to top up their glasses. When he realised the glasses were still full, he set it back down again. He rolled his shoulders and scowled. 'It must've been the same for you. You said your mother left when you were six. That means Danny was still a baby. You practically raised him.'

'Not single-handedly. There was my father and Uncle Archie. Grandma was still alive then. Yes, my mother left and it was hard and awful—I missed her so much. But, Simon, I always felt I had family around, people who loved me. Felice, she had no one but you.'

Across the table, Simon met Kate's eyes. Her concern made his awkwardness disappear. He could see the morbid fancies she painted in her mind and it screwed him up tight. He didn't want her wasting her sympathy on him.

'Felice and I had each other. We did okay.' Yet he'd managed to ruin even that.

'And now?' Kate whispered.

A crippling weight crashed down on his shoulders. 'And now we don't.' And it was all his fault.

'What happened, Simon? I can tell you were close. I can tell it was you who read her bedtime stories, bandaged scraped knees and kept her entertained when she had the flu. You probably even went to the open days at her school.'

He had, whenever he'd been able to manage.

She lifted an eyebrow, but it didn't judge him; it just asked the question—what happened?

Simon frowned. 'It all suddenly became too bloody hard!' he burst out, surprising even himself with his vehemence.

'Too hard…?'

'She started talking about becoming a ski instructor. Do you know what happens on the ski fields?' he demanded.

Wordlessly, Kate shook her head.

'Well…it isn't pretty,' he shot back. 'Avalanches, broken legs… Seductions!' French and Italian men could be smooth. They could turn a young girl's head, break her heart. He could feel his scowl darkening his whole face, but he couldn't help it. 'Then she went and found herself a boyfriend with a motorbike. Do you know how dangerous that is?'

'Um…'

'Then, get this, she and her girlfriends would go out on the town clubbing and—' he leaned towards her '—they'd walk home at some ridiculous time in the morning instead of catching a cab. In London!' Felice had been furious the few times he'd waited outside a nightclub to escort her home. 'She wouldn't listen to a damn word I said.' In fact, as soon as he said one thing, she'd go and do the opposite.

'It was hard enough keeping her out of trouble when she was ten. How was I supposed to do that once she turned eighteen?'

'You're not supposed to. You step back and let her fend for herself.'

She reached out and touched his hand briefly, fleetingly. Somehow it soothed him.

'You hope you've instilled enough natural caution and good values in them to get them through. Then you let them fly free.'

She sat back and he shook his head. He hadn't been able to do that. Felice was so young, so vulnerable.

'And you stand by, ready to pick up the pieces if it all comes crashing down around them.'

No, he wanted to avert crashes. Felice did not deserve crashes.

'You did a good job of raising her, Simon. She's a lovely young woman—natural, well-adjusted and more than capable of making her own decisions. Which is remarkable, given your parents' attitude and absence. I think that's wholly down to you. She always had your unconditional love. She had one person in her life she could always rely on.'

'If that's true, she wouldn't have run away from me.' Acid burned his throat. He'd driven her away and failed her—the final proof that fatherhood was beyond him.

'Oh, what a load of piffle!' Kate's tone had him swinging to face her. 'Run away from you? You're her brother, not her father. Stop acting like one and start acting like the other again.' She pointed her index finger at him. 'If you don't, you may just find she will never speak to you again.'

His mouth opened and closed, but he couldn't think of a single thing to say.

'How do you think you'd react if someone told you that you weren't capable of running your estate and started vetting your dates and demanding you be home by midnight? I can't see you submitting to that.'

Neither could he.

'Well, why should Felice?'

'But she's only…'

'Twenty-two! Last time I checked, that's old enough to vote, old enough to have babies and old enough to decide what to do with the rest of your life. What were you doing at twenty-two?'

At university, living his own life.

His shoulders suddenly slumped. Twenty-two? Was Felice really twenty-two? He sighed heavily. He'd done everything he could to check her freedom. Everything. And it hadn't just been in an attempt to keep her safe, he saw now with a clarity that sickened and shamed him. He hadn't wanted her to stretch her wings and leave him all alone. The way he'd been alone before she'd been born.

He'd left her no choice but to run away.

In the light that spilled from the house, he saw Kate's face soften. 'Oh, Simon, do you really think—given your history and everything you know about Felice—that you can't make things right again?'

He stared at her. 'You mean if I apologise to Felice and stop trying to boss her around, then things might be okay between us again?'

'That's exactly what I mean.'

He opened his mouth. He closed it. He scratched his hands back through his hair. And then it hit him. She was right. About Felice—about him.

When had he lost his sense of proportion?

In the darkness their gazes met and held. Somehow this remarkable woman had burrowed beneath all his defences. And he couldn't even find it in himself to regret it. His father in particular would've found that admission unforgivable. Poor form was what he'd have called it. Simon didn't care. For the first time in his adult life, he didn't give two hoots for what his parents would've thought or for what duty demanded. The fear that had taken him over in the past few months, persecuting him with guilt and regret, had gone. The relief of it flowed through him, making him feel like a new man.

It was all because of Kate. Because she cared about people with a warmth and generosity he'd never encountered in anyone before. She gave without a thought for getting anything in return. She was so damn easy to talk to.

And kiss.

That thought, with all of its associated memories, flitted through his mind and lodged there.

'Simon?'

He dragged himself back from thoughts of kissing her, touching her. No, dammit, he would touch her. He reached across and clasped her hand. 'If I apologise, Felice will forgive me.'

'Yes.' Her generous lips lifted into an even more generous smile. She squeezed his hand.

'She's an adult. I need to treat her like an adult.'

'It won't be easy,' she warned.

'No, but I can do it.' He had to do it.

Kate's smile widened.

'She might even want to help me run the businesses attached to the estate. With a little training, she'd be a whiz at PR and marketing. Perhaps she'd even like to take over the—'

'Simon!'

Her smile had faded. He shrugged sheepishly. 'I'm getting carried away, aren't I?'

'Yes.'

She didn't spare him and he appreciated that.

'Felice may not want to work for the estate. She might still want to become a ski instructor.' She worried at her bottom lip. 'And, if she does, you will have to respect that.'

Kate was right. Again. He could no longer force his will on Felice. Not if he wanted to rebuild their relationship. But the woman sitting opposite him, the woman whose hand trembled in his, had given him hope that it could be rebuilt.

'You are a remarkable woman, Kate Petherbridge.' Before he knew what he was about, he'd drawn her to her feet. 'You are kind and wise and more generous than any soul I've ever met.'

'Don't be silly.'

Her words emerged on a throaty whisper that brushed across his skin, sensitizing it. It made him aware of the cooling air on his face and the contrasting fire starting to burn low in the pit of his stomach. A fire he feared only this woman could quench.

'Simon?'

That throaty whisper again. He couldn't move away. The pulse at the base of her throat pounded wildly against her silver dolphin charm, and all Simon could think of was brushing that charm aside and closing his mouth over that spot and laving it with his tongue, grazing it with his teeth. Tasting her, breathing her deep into his lungs.

He reached out and cupped her face...and she let him. His sense of wonder, of privilege, built.

Dazed eyes met his. 'You really have hit holiday-maker mode, haven't you?'

'If I have, it's down to you.' He brushed his thumb across her cheek and her breath quickened. 'You've helped me find my sense of proportion. I know that much.'

Her eyes softened. 'You're a smart man, Simon.' Her hand came up to curl around his wrist. 'You'd have found it on your own eventually.'

She didn't pull her hand away. She left it there. The blood throbbed through his veins, hard and insistent. 'You are remarkable *and* amazing.' He meant every word.

But she wasn't looking into his eyes any more. Her gaze had lowered to his lips. Her chest rose and fell, outlining curves that were sweet and inviting. He couldn't help himself. He lowered his head and brushed his mouth across her lips—reverently, softly. She smelt of all things golden—sunshine and lemons, summer and Chardonnay.

She trembled. He drew back and eventually she opened her eyes. ' I think you're pretty terrific too,' she whispered.

She reached up and kissed him back—just as softly, just as reverently—but this time Simon couldn't let her go. He curved a hand around the back of her head, slid his fingers into the satin of her hair and deepened the kiss. Slowly at first, but thoroughly, taking his time to learn the exact shape of her mouth, the texture of her lips. Drawing her along without haste, giving to her the way she'd given to him. She melted against him, wound her arms around his neck and all her softness melted into all his hardness and he wanted—needed—to touch and taste every part of her.

Her soft moans as he pressed kisses to her neck thrilled him. Her fingers curving into his shoulders urged him closer. He slid his fingers under her shirt and she arched into him as he moved to cup her breasts through the thin cotton of her bra. He groaned as her nipples hardened against his palm.

She was perfect! Wonderful and perfect.

With a growl, she tugged his T-shirt over his head and Simon suddenly found that he was the one whose body was wracked by shivers, who had to grind back cries as her fingers travelled over the planes and angles of his chest and back…stomach…her mouth and tongue following until he couldn't stand it any longer and he had to drag her mouth back to his for hot, hungry kisses. He couldn't get enough of her. He'd never get enough of her. He needed her the way he needed air and water. His last hope…

Hope? The word filtered into his consciousness.

Needed? The word nagged at him.

No!

He seized her arms and put her from him. He tried to bite back a groan when her lip-swollen, kiss-dazed face lifted to his. When he sensed she'd found her balance he released her. 'I'm sorry, Kate, but this can't happen.'

The words came out loud and harsh. He didn't mean them to, and what was worse was that he knew she'd know that. He seized his shirt from the ground and hauled it back over his head, willing the cool night air to dampen the fever raging through him.

This was how he thanked her? Oh, well done! Things had gone well beyond a holiday fling and into realms that threatened to blow his mind.

He didn't want his damn mind blown.

If she lived in England, he'd consider exploring where this might take them. Maybe.

He glanced at her. There was no maybe about it. This woman could come to mean more to him than any other person on the planet.

He raked his hands back over his head, digging his fingers into his scalp. God, she had a child. He couldn't explore anything with her. He didn't mess with single mothers. Kate Petherbridge was kind and giving, and she sure as hell didn't deserve to be messed about by the likes of him.

He would be no good for her.

'Relax, Simon.' She drew in a shuddering breath. 'It was… just a kiss.'

He didn't know who she was trying to convince, but he refused to play along. 'It wasn't just a kiss. We nearly…' He couldn't finish the sentence, couldn't look at her.

Kate moved away from him then, all the way around the table until it stood between them. Then she sat in the seat furthest away from him. He'd said she was wise, hadn't he?

'Yes, you're right.'

Her voice held no emotion. She clutched her glass of wine in both hands, but she didn't bring it up to her lips. She looked utterly miserable. Remorse speared through him, and regret. He hooked out the nearest chair and fell into it. 'I'm sorry,' he repeated.

'Me too.'

Her? She had nothing to apologise for. He closed his eyes and hardened his heart. 'But at the risk of sounding like a broken-down record,' he ground out.

'Yes.' She nodded. 'You and me, we'd never make it work.' She touched the glass of wine to her cheek as if welcoming its coolness, but she still didn't take a sip. 'Jesse.'

That single word dropped into the silence between them.

'It's not just Jesse, Kate.' Simon shook is head. 'I have too many commitments in England. Inheritance tax, for a start.'

She roused herself enough to look at him. 'Inheritance tax?'

'When my father died, the estate was crippled by the inheritance tax.' He wondered if his weariness showed. It hadn't helped that the sixth Lord of Holm had completely mismanaged the estate's funds either. Simon's lips twisted. His father had liked spending money but hadn't been quite so keen on earning it. He rubbed a hand across his eyes. 'When my father died, I had to take out a loan to cover the cost of the inheritance tax. The loan is guaranteed by the businesses I run from the estate. I'm tied to it now for at least ten years.'

She eyed him over the rim of her glass. 'The only way you can pay back this loan is by running these businesses of yours from the estate?'

He nodded heavily. 'The businesses are tied to the estate. We've opened up the house to the public and we're turning the main wing into a convention centre. Apparently we're going to be quite popular with the wedding market. Old houses with established gardens are apparently all the rage.'

'And you're honour bound to pay off this loan.'

'Yes.' He'd promised the bank manager and the people who depended on the estate for their livelihoods that he'd see it through.

Amazingly, she smiled at him then. 'And you're not the kind of man who'd break his word.'

He hoped not.

'I admire that.' She glanced down into her glass of untouched wine and her smile disappeared. 'Can you give me your word that…that—' she gestured to the spot where they'd kissed '—won't happen again?'

It hit him then that he couldn't.

'Because, Simon, I don't think I can,' she blurted out. 'I lose all sense of reason when I'm around you.' She took one sip of her wine, then set the glass on the table. 'I don't want to, but my hormones keep taking over.'

She had his full sympathy.

'Which is why I'm going to take myself off to bed right now.'

She pushed her chair back and moved towards the house. Simon forced himself to remain where he was. 'Goodnight, Kate.'

Her, 'Goodnight, Simon,' drifted back to him on the warm night air.

When he was sure she was gone, he reached across and captured her glass in his fingers, placed his lips to the same spot hers had been and tried to drag some scent of her from the glass. It didn't work. All he could smell was the soft, woody scent of an aged Chardonnay.

CHAPTER SEVEN

'WHERE'S Simon?'

Kate's heart squeezed at the anticipation lighting her young son's face. 'Still in bed, chook.'

If he were anything like her, Simon would have spent most of the night tossing and turning, tangled in longing and plagued by what-ifs. If he'd fallen asleep in the wee small hours, she and Jesse would do their best not to disturb him.

'What a sleepyhead!'

'Just like you when you're on holiday,' she teased, setting a cereal bowl and spoon in front of him.

And if Simon weren't asleep it'd mean he was avoiding her. She shook herself and tried to do cheerful and chipper. 'If you want to walk to school with Nick and his mum, you'd better get a move on, mister.' Flora was on another health kick. Walking the kids to and from school formed part of her new exercise regime.

Kate sipped her coffee, staring out of the kitchen window at another perfect day. She resented the sun for shining so brightly, the sky for refusing admittance to grey clouds and the bay for appearing so darn calm and unruffled. If Simon weren't asleep…

It'd mean he'd stay holed up in his room until she left for work.

Which was a good thing, she tried to tell herself, because the effects of last night's kiss lingered too vividly in her mind. She hadn't got over it yet and her body clamoured for a replay.

She needed more time to get her traitorous flesh—her traitorous mind—back under control. Last night she'd been ready to give him everything. He didn't want everything. Not from her, at least. And he liked her too much to pretend otherwise. Seeing him this morning would not help.

It didn't stop her from wanting to see him.

'Mum?'

Something in Jesse's tone told her it wasn't the first time he'd called her. She spun from the window. 'Sorry, chook, I was a million miles away.'

He held up his bowl. 'I've finished.'

His blue eyes were filled with concern and Kate berated herself for worrying him. 'Woo hoo!' she cheered, and didn't care if Simon was asleep or not, if he heard or not. He didn't deserve sleep. He deserved to be as frustrated and tied up in knots as she was. She pasted on a big grin, kissed the top of her son's head and whisked away his bowl. 'Well done, champ. Now go and get dressed.'

Jesse's face cleared and with a whoop he raced off to his bedroom.

By the time Jesse left for school the perfect day outside had simply become even more perfect. She scowled at it. It wasn't like she wanted a spectacular thunderstorm. Grey would do. Her shoulders drooped, her mouth drooped, even her eyes drooped.

Then she heard the door to Simon's room open and she snapped to attention—all droopiness gone, all resentment at the perfect weather forgotten.

How could she look him in the face?

How could she not?

One thing became abundantly clear—putting it off would only make it worse. She forced her legs to carry her to the arched doorway that led down the hall to his room. She stopped one pace short, pulled in a breath, rehearsed asking him if he wanted coffee, then forced herself forward again…

And practically collided with him. 'Oh, Simon! I thought I heard you.'

Tanned hands reached out to steady her, his fingers curling into the flesh of her upper arms—the bare flesh—and she couldn't move away. She gazed up at him with the same helplessness as she had last night. The fire he'd lit inside her burst back into being.

It was Simon who took the step back, who let his hands drop. Just like he had last night. Even though the hunger in his face matched hers.

She swallowed. 'Coffee?'

She closed her eyes, mortified at the huskiness of her voice. Coffee? It had sounded more like an offer to go to bed. She kinked open one eye to find him shaking his head. Then he motioned down the hallway to the front door.

She blinked. And, although she hadn't thought it possible to feel any worse today, when she saw Simon's suitcase sitting neat and upright at the end of the hallway, she knew she'd been wrong.

'You're leaving?' The sight of the suitcase annihilated any trace of huskiness from her voice.

'Yes.'

'But Felice…'

'I've booked into the Bayside Hotel.'

It was just down the road. 'It's good,' she found herself saying.

He took her hand. 'I thank you from the bottom of my heart for your hospitality.'

She couldn't say anything. He squeezed her hand. Then he turned and headed for the front door.

'No!' She raced down the hall, set her hand against the door and pushed it shut. 'Surely this isn't necessary?'

He couldn't leave. She didn't want him to leave.

He had to leave for England in another week.

'Kate.' He touched her face, drew her eyes to his. 'You asked me last night if I could promise not to kiss you again. I can't.'

She did her very, very best to stop the blood from chugging through her veins with unadulterated excitement.

'This thing between us is stronger than my sense of right and wrong. You have given me so much.'

She wanted to melt under the warmth of his eyes. If only he'd let her give him more.

'You're kind and generous and more caring than any person I've ever met. If I stay in your house, if I kiss you one more time, I will hurt you. I don't want that. You don't deserve that. You deserve better than wham, bam, thank you, ma'am.'

Yes, she did.

And he had to return to England.

If he gave in to this attraction, the protective side of his nature would see it as evidence of another failure.

She removed her hand from the door.

She couldn't speak. She could only nod.

He leant down, brushing his lips across her forehead, and left. His scent lingered. She stood in the doorway long after his car had disappeared to breathe him in.

As if in a dream, she turned and walked back down the hallway and into the guest room—Simon's room. She eased herself down onto the bed. A shudder racked her body as she buried her face in the covers. Her throat burned. Her eyes burned.

She didn't know how long she lay there, but finally she forced herself upright and out of the room. She returned to the kitchen, seized her handbag and let herself out of the back door. She set off towards the marina. She had a business to run.

Simon filled his lungs with salt-drenched air, then took in the lengthening shadows, the utter stillness that had descended over Dutchman's Bay. Not even the leaves on the flame trees moved and he knew he could grow as addicted as Kate to these late summer afternoons. His heart dipped. Not that it would do him any good. Once he'd sorted things out with Felice he would have to return to England. Leave Kate and her beautiful summer evenings behind.

His hotel sat just above the beach. From his room he had a

view of the bay, but not of Kate's house—her beautiful, ram-shackle, comfortable house. So he sat on the beach where he could see it.

He leant back on his hands, the sand beneath them warm, but the warmth couldn't penetrate the chill that surrounded his heart. It didn't matter which way he looked at it—he didn't want to leave Kate.

He ground his teeth together, curled his hands into the sand. He would leave, though. Kate deserved a better man than him.

A child's shout broke the stillness.

Jesse?

He turned to find Jesse racing along the beach towards him, three other kids in tow. Nick was one of them. In the park, Flora sat on a bench with a couple of other women. She raised her hand. He waved back.

Then he caught the cricket ball Jesse tossed at him before it slammed into his nose. 'Wotcha doing down here, Simon?'

'Soaking up some rays. What are you doing down here?'

'Waiting for Mum.'

Simon wondered if that was what he was doing too. He knew she walked home this way. He couldn't get thoughts of her out of his head. Those thoughts wouldn't do him any good, though. He jerked his head to the hotel behind them. 'I've just moved in there.'

'Why?' Jesse's face screwed up for a moment and his eyes narrowed. 'Have you had a fight with Mum?'

'No!' He tried to moderate his tone. 'Nothing like that. Can you imagine anyone fighting with your mum?'

'Nah, except Uncle Danny sometimes and they're not real fights but tiffs.'

Simon grinned. He could hear Kate in just about every word of that sentence.

'Besides,' Jesse added, 'fights between brothers and sisters don't count.'

Out of the mouths of babes… Simon hoped Jesse was right.

'Do you and Auntie Felice fight?'

Felice was an honorary aunt, was she? It made Simon grin. 'You bet. And your auntie Felice will need her old room back soon, which is why I've moved out.'

'Oh. Okay.'

And apparently that was all the explanation necessary. Jesse turned to his companions. 'This is Simon who I told you about. The one who plays cricket.'

'Well…he might know,' one of Jesse's companions said.

'Know what?' Simon couldn't help asking.

Jesse heaved an exaggerated sigh. 'How to make the cricket ball spin that way instead of that way.'

Simon rolled his eyes and wondered how many kids the world over had been seduced by the glamour of famous spin bowlers. 'I prefer fast bowling,' he muttered.

'Us too,' Jesse said glumly. 'But Nick's mum said we had to play nicely…gently.'

Simon bit back a grin. He weighed the ball in his hands then leapt to his feet. 'Look, you need to hold the ball like this.' He demonstrated. 'But it takes a lot of practice,' he warned as they all gathered around. 'Here—' he handed the ball to Jesse '—you try.'

Kate heard Jesse in the park well before she could see him. It made her step lighten a little. She and Jesse were doing just fine. They didn't need some English lord type coming in to make everything right and good. Everything was already right and good.

And if she told herself that often enough, eventually it would become fact.

The problem was, it had been fact before Simon had come back-flipping into her world and made her feel like a princess.

She pushed that thought away and focused instead on her child's laughter. Jesse—the one uncomplicated blessing in her life. She rounded the final bend in the path and her eyes landed on Jesse first.

Simon second.

It took a while before she noticed the other children, the park bench of mothers. The shadows were long, the air warm and tinged orange and blue and...

Simon? Her gaze swung back. Simon was playing cricket. With Jesse. On the beach.

'Hey, Mum!'

Jesse waved but he didn't race away from his game to throw his arms around her waist and hug her. The other children stopped the game long enough to wave at her too. She waved back. Simon just stared. She knew exactly how clear the grey of those eyes would be. She wanted to race across and throw herself into his arms.

Um...Jesse, children, other mothers...not a good time to throw herself at anyone.

Finally he nodded.

Kate couldn't manage even that much. She staggered over to the park bench and collapsed beside Flora.

'Big day, love?' Flora tutted in sympathy.

Kate nodded. 'You could say that.'

The next afternoon, Kate found herself confronted with a similar scene. Simon in the park. Again. Playing cricket with Jesse and Nick. And it suddenly occurred to her that a dangerous precedent was threatening to form. What the hell did Simon think he was doing?

She passed a hand across her eyes. Thank heavens it was Friday. Paul would collect Jesse in approximately two hours and Jesse would be away at his dad's for the entire weekend. That would nip this crazy situation in the bud.

She waved to Jesse and Nick. She tried to nod at Simon.

Oh, good Lord. He was wearing those Hawaiian print board shorts she'd insisted he buy on that first day. She remembered the digging of feet into sand, the feeding of seagulls and the walking on hands.

She remembered the pressure of his lips on hers—the wonderful exhilaration and freedom of it.

She couldn't nod. Instead she took a seat beside Flora.

'Heavens, love, you look done in. What you need is a holiday.'

She remembered saying those exact same words to Simon.

'Perhaps when Danny gets back,' the other woman said kindly.

'Perhaps.' She did her best to raise a smile. When Danny got back Simon would leave. What use would a holiday be to her then?

When Kate rounded the last bend in the path the following Monday and took in the scene—Simon, Jesse and Nick playing cricket yet again—she knew she would have to do something to bring this afternoon ritual to an end.

How many hearts did Simon mean to break?

'Garbage,' she ground out under her breath. Simon hadn't broken her heart. No sirree. She slumped onto the bench beside Flora and glowered at Simon, at the bay, at the sky. Her heart was intact, thank you very much, and that was how Jesse's would remain too.

'You're muttering, love.'

Kate crashed back with a bump. 'Was I?' Good Lord, how embarrassing. 'Sorry.'

'Still…it's an improvement.'

Kate stared at Flora, feeling vaguely appalled. 'Over what?'

'Over all that dog-tired depression.'

'I haven't been depressed!' She hadn't. No way!

Flora stared at her, then glanced at Simon and lifted an eyebrow. Kate bit back a groan and waited for some pithy observation—something along the lines of, *You wouldn't be the first girl to tie yourself in knots over a man.*

And not just any man but a tourist too. The locals took a pretty dim view when it came to tourists. The tourists were fine to have fun with, but you didn't pin your hopes on them. A body didn't get much sympathy if a tourist broke their heart, not around here.

Because a girl should know better.

But that kiss…

That rotten, wonderful, fly in the face of everything she ever thought she knew kiss.

Flora didn't make any kind of pithy observation. She simply said, 'I promised the boys they could make chocolate crackles this afternoon.'

'You're brave. It'll take you a week to clean your kitchen.' Then she drew back to gaze at Flora. 'Didn't I say you needed to incorporate chocolate into that new-fangled diet of yours?' Flora must be getting antsy if she was prepared to let the boys loose in her kitchen.

By 'boys' Kate took her to mean Jesse and Nick, not Simon. Nobody could describe Simon as a boy. Not with those strong abs and powerful thighs. She shook herself, reminding herself about not muttering.

'Hence the chocolate crackles,' Flora confessed, 'And one chocolate crackle seems a whole lot less fatal to my diet than an entire packet of biscuits.'

'True, and you can freeze chocolate crackles, you know?' For emergencies. Kate wondered if she had any chocolate in the house.

Flora rubbed her hands together. 'I know.'

The glee in her eyes made Kate laugh. Then she noticed how intently Jesse watched Simon as Simon demonstrated some complicated bowling action, as Simon took the young boy's arm to correct his technique and demonstrate what he meant, and her laughter dried up. Hero-worship oozed from each and every one of her son's pores.

'I'll take the boys home.' Flora patted Kate's hand. 'And I think you should sit here and soak up the…' her eyes rested on Simon '…view.'

Kate straightened from her slouch. It'd give her a chance to tackle Simon about Jesse. 'I'd like that,' she said carefully. 'Are you sure?'

'Oh, yes.' Flora rose. 'I'm on a chocolate crackle crusade.'

With that, she called the boys and disappeared. Suddenly the park was quiet again. Too quiet. Simon hesitated, then moved towards her. Kate leapt off the bench. Sitting with Simon seemed somehow way too cosy. He was leaving in another week. Probably less.

She wasn't getting cosy with Simon. Not again.

'Hello, Kate.'

'What the hell do you think you're doing?' Until the words shot out of her, she hadn't realised the throb and burn of the anger coursing through her.

Perhaps it wasn't anger at all, but…frustration? Physical, body-yearning frustration. That thought didn't improve her mood either.

Simon's head jerked back. That mask of his slipped into place and she wanted to slap it away. 'Would you like to be a little more explicit?'

Ooh, she'd give him explicit all right. 'Try playing with my son's feelings on for size,' she snapped.

He took a step back. Colour drained from his face. 'You want me to stop playing cricket with Jesse?'

'Last week you would barely give him the time of day. This week you're all friendly and making him love you when you'll be gone in a few days. Do you call that fair?'

He'd leave and forget all about them.

Consternation replaced his surprise. Hurt flashed across his face so briefly she wondered if she'd imagined it. At the same moment, her anger fizzled away.

'I…I didn't realise.'

She wanted to cry. She wanted to hug him. Neither one of those reactions could possibly be construed as appropriate.

'What do you want me to do?'

Stay. She wanted him to stay. She stared at him, appalled, as the knowledge pounded through her. She wanted him to stay. But he couldn't.

Simon set his shoulders. 'I'll make sure I'm not here

tomorrow. And Wednesday, I'll be here briefly because I'd hate him to think I've forgotten him, but I'll make some excuse and I won't play cricket with him. I'll ease back.'

He'd done his best to keep his voice even, but the ache behind it almost undid her.

'Kate, I wouldn't hurt you or yours for the world.'

'I know.'

She had so much and he had so little. Even if he succeeded in patching things up with Felice, he had in a sense already lost her. Not that he knew that yet. And now she'd made him feel bad about caring for Jesse.

'Don't even think that,' she said vehemently, recognising the lines of defeat in his shoulders. And his eyes. His beautiful grey eyes. 'This is *not* more proof that you're a failure with kids. Over the last few days everything you've done with Jesse has been perfect.'

It was true. *If* he was staying…

But he wasn't.

'Perfect,' she repeated. 'It's just happening at the wrong time in the wrong place.'

She reached up on tiptoe and kissed his cheek because she couldn't help it. Because in all likelihood this would be the last time she'd ever see him on his own. Ever.

Simon watched Kate walk away. He touched the spot on his cheek where the imprint of lips burned. He wanted to race after her, haul her into his arms and to hell with the consequences.

But something told him the consequences would be too big. He didn't care for himself. But Kate? Kate deserved something better.

He swung away. He couldn't stand the sight of her walking away from him. He'd removed himself from her house. She was removing him from the rest of her life. It was only wise and right.

He headed down onto the sand and kicked off his flip-flops, twisting his body until sand covered his feet to the ankles. It didn't help. Not this time. Not a single ounce of tension eased out of him.

With an oath, he threw himself down on the sand to rest his arms on bent knees. He stared moodily out at the bay—calm and smooth—but none of its tranquillity could ease his turmoil. Kate wanted him to stop playing with Jesse. A second hole opened up somewhere in the region of his chest. She wanted him to stop spending time with Jesse. Rightly so, he reminded himself, but he hadn't known it would make him feel...

Bereft. Like he was already grieving.

Somewhere along the line something inside him had changed. He'd played cricket with Jesse that first day in the park here because there'd been mothers—responsible adults—nearby. Mothers who would puff up at him if he did anything wrong—like Kate had just done, like the mother of his little god-daughter had done. He'd played with Jesse that first day because he hadn't been able to get Kate out of his mind. But all the days after that, he hadn't noticed the mothers. When playing with Jesse, he hadn't thought about Kate—Jesse's non-stop chatter and the exercise had seen to that.

Without trying too hard, he'd formed an easy, relaxed friendship with Jesse. He'd started to grow fond of the little boy, love him, because he was so damn easy to love.

Were all children like that?

Everything you've done with Jesse has been perfect. Kate's words sounded through him.

Wrong place. Wrong time.

Perfect.

He leapt up. He started to pace. Could Kate be right about this too? Hope he'd never allowed himself to feel started hammering at defences he'd erected a long time ago. Could he have children of his own?

Perfect.

Yes, he could! The knowledge poured into him—a gift. Kate was right. He *could* have children. He *would* have children. He wanted those children with a fierceness he didn't try to check or suppress or deny.

Yet…there was only one woman he wanted to have those children with. He swung in the direction of her house…of her. He had to tell her. Now.

He started to jog. Falling in love with Kate, learning to love Jesse—there could never be a wrong time or wrong place for that. He started to pick up speed, his legs eating up the distance as he hurtled towards the stairs that led up to her house. He had to tell her she was perfect for him. He had to convince her he was perfect for her. He had to convince her to take a chance on them.

'Kate!'

Kate swung around and almost fell over at the sight of Simon at her back door. He stepped inside, his chest heaving as if he'd sprinted up here as fast as he could from the beach—like Jesse did sometimes.

Alarm dashed through her. 'What is it?' She raced over and shook his arm. 'What's happened?'

'Nothing,' he panted. 'I've just come to my senses and I had to tell you—'

He broke off to rest his hands on his knees. What did he have to tell her?

'It hit me, you see, then I had to get up here as fast as I could…and now…just got to catch my breath,' he wheezed, gesturing to his chest. 'Out of condition.'

Fiddlesticks. Simon Morton-Blake was lean and dreamboat-hard. She knew. She'd had a full body imprint.

Not a good thought, she realised when her blood started to chug. If it didn't slow down she'd be resting her hands on her knees and breathing hard too.

After three deep breaths he straightened and his hands descended to her shoulders. At the look in his eyes her blood started to bubble. He opened his mouth. She couldn't drag her eyes from those lean, firm lips. Lips that had taken her to heights she hadn't known she could scale. Lips that had uttered words in exactly the right way.

'I…' He swallowed. 'Er…'

Except now.

'Verisimilitude,' she whispered.

He gazed at her blankly. 'I beg your pardon?'

Yes, he said that perfectly too. 'Just say it,' she ordered. Well, she meant it to be an order but it came out more like a plea. If she had to beg, so be it. She may never hear that word uttered in this exact same fashion ever again.

His brows drew together. 'Verisimilitude.'

Ooh, yes. A girl could swoon under the influence of that accent.

Simon's brow suddenly cleared and he seized her shoulders again. 'Kate, I—'

The front door crashed open and Kate's name was piped through the house in an accent identical to Simon's, only female.

Simon's jaw dropped. Then he grinned. 'Felice?'

Kate nodded. The moment she'd dreaded had finally arrived. Simon would leave Nelson's Bay—perhaps as soon as tomorrow. And he probably wouldn't even like her any more.

It shouldn't matter.

But somehow it mattered more than anything else in the world.

CHAPTER EIGHT

FELICE burst into the room and the moment Simon's eyes landed on her they lit up. A shaft of pain slid between Kate's ribs. Felice's news would hurt him. She wanted to prevent anything from ever hurting him again. She knew that was ridiculous, impossible even.

With a startled squeak, Felice slid to a halt.

'Hey, sis,' Danny said, coming up behind Felice.

'Danny.' She swallowed as she watched him glance from Simon to Felice. Nobody said anything. Kate cleared her throat. 'Simon, this is my brother, Danny. Um…Danny, this is Simon…'

'Felice's brother,' he finished for her. He stuck out a hand. 'Hi.'

'Pleased to meet you,' Simon said automatically, shaking it.

But his eyes had only lifted from Felice's face for a fraction of a second before returning. Kate's heart bled a little more. She'd never seen Felice wear that shuttered expression before. When she folded her arms, she looked completely closed up.

'I didn't expect to find you still here, Simon.'

No hello, no kiss on the cheek.

'I wanted to make sure you were okay.'

No frown or scowl, no roll of his shoulders, but the grey of his eyes darkened to the colour of charcoal.

Felice snorted. 'Wanted to make sure I wasn't dragging the family name in the mud, more like.'

Kate jumped in. 'I talked Simon into taking advantage of the fabulous weather and having a holiday.'

Felice's eyes boggled. 'A holiday?' She stared at Simon. 'You?'

He grinned, but Kate sensed the effort behind it. 'I decided to follow your lead. I have to say you're onto something, Felice. I wish I'd listened to you earlier.'

Felice's jaw dropped. With a visible effort, she hauled it back up. Then her eyes narrowed, her shoulders went back and Kate knew exactly what the younger girl meant to hurl at him.

No! She clapped her hands. They had to give him more time. All eyes turned to her and she forced a smile. 'I wasn't expecting you guys before Wednesday.'

Danny's hand curled around Felice's. As Kate backed up towards the coffee machine, too afraid to take her eyes off any of them, Simon's smoky gaze zeroed in on those linked hands. But she'd told him about that. That shouldn't surprise him. She wished she'd found a better way to prepare him for what was to come.

'Felice felt bad that we left you in the lurch.'

Simon blinked at Danny's words. 'And did you leave Kate in the lurch?'

Danny grinned at Kate. 'Yes and no.' Then he winked.

Relief threaded through her. This she could handle. 'As you can see, we're utterly run off our feet. All hands on deck and whatnot. We even put Simon to work one weekend.'

Felice's jaw dropped again. Danny nudged her. 'See? I said you were worried about nothing.'

'Coffee everyone?' She had to perform contortions to pour coffee beans into the machine without turning her back on anyone. They could all sit around the kitchen table like civilised adults, share some innocuous news, and then she'd drag Danny off so Simon and Felice could talk alone.

She wished she was psychic, wished Danny and Felice were too so she could send that suggestion—command—straight to their brains.

Felice's face hardened as her initial shock wore off. Her chin lifted in determination. 'Coffee? Oh, no, we've something much better than that.'

Kate knew she couldn't stop what was about to come. She wanted to yell at Felice to be gentle.

'We bought champagne!' Her high tinkling laugh reverberated in Kate's head, making it throb. 'To celebrate.'

Simon's forehead furrowed. 'Celebrate?'

Kate wanted to cry when she watched him clear his frown and do what he could to replace it with a smile. 'What are we celebrating?'

Kate closed her eyes.

Felice continued in a hard voice Kate found difficult to associate with her. 'I'm hoping you'll toast my marriage to Danny.'

Kate opened her eyes. Even behind her defiance, Felice's happiness lit up the whole room as effectively as the sun did each morning. Envy surged through Kate. And yearning.

With a swallow, she turned her head the tiniest fraction. Simon's brow furrowed again. He dragged a hand back through his hair. 'Married?'

Kate barely recognised his voice. Felice held up her left hand to display her simple gold wedding band. The tan leached from his face and Kate wanted to yell at Felice and Danny—*You haven't given him enough time!*

She wanted to grab Simon's arm and beg him not to say anything unforgivable, anything that would widen the breach between him and his sister.

He turned, speared her with his gaze. 'You knew about this?'

'Yes.' The admission croaked from her.

His eyes blazed. 'And you didn't think to mention it to me?'

'I thought Felice needed to be the one to tell you.'

'You *thought*—' His voice rose. 'Well, you thought *wrong*!'

He'd trusted her, and she'd betrayed that trust. For a moment she thought she might be sick.

'Don't go firing up at Kate,' Felice shot at him. 'She's been nothing but kind and supportive and too lovely for words. And don't bother starting in on Danny either,' she added when Simon opened his mouth again. 'He didn't even know I had a family, let alone a wealthy, titled one, until after we'd married.'

Simon's lips tightened. 'Starting married life off with a lie? Why would I expect anything less of you, Felice?'

Felice started to shake with what Kate suspected was barely suppressed anger. 'Marrying Danny is the one good thing I've done with my life. I love him more than life itself and I know he loves me too. Danny and Kate, they don't care about things like what family a person comes from or how much money they have.'

'I know.'

Felice's shaking stopped. 'You do?'

'I've spent nearly a week and a half in Kate's company. It took less than an hour before I knew without question that she had decency and integrity. I would expect the same of the brother she had a hand in raising.'

Kate couldn't read the expression in his eyes, but she sensed the pain rolling through him. He might think she had decency and integrity, but it didn't change the fact that he felt betrayed by her.

'From all I've heard, Felice, you're a lucky woman.' His face remained immobile, wooden. 'Congratulations. I hope you'll both be very happy.'

'So...so you'll share a glass of champagne with us?'

'No.' He shook his head. 'You'll have to excuse me.' He moved towards the back door.

'So you don't wish us happiness.'

It was a statement, not a question. Simon turned from the door. 'If you'd wanted me to toast you, Felice, you'd have invited me to your wedding.'

'Get over yourself, Si. We didn't invite anyone to our wedding. We didn't have one. We eloped.'

Felice said the words with a studied casualness that Kate saw through. She wondered if Simon did too.

'We didn't tell anyone, not even Kate, until after the event. In fact, until now she's the only other person who knew. So you needn't think we were playing favourites.'

'Eloped?' Simon took two steps back into the room. He turned to Kate and a flush of anger crossed his face. 'So you hurt her too?' He swung back to Felice. 'After all the kindness and friendship she's shown you, that's how you treat her?'

Felice gripped Danny's arm. 'We didn't! We didn't hurt your feelings, did we, Kate?'

'I...' She didn't want to make Felice feel bad, but she couldn't lie when Simon's smoky eyes glared at her like that. 'I'd have given anything to see my brother married to the woman he loved,' she admitted.

Felice's hands went to her lips. 'I'm sorry,' she whispered.

Kate dredged up a smile. 'I know.'

Then she turned and met Simon's glare with one of her own. She folded her arms and raised an eyebrow.

'What?' he suddenly exploded. 'You still want me to apologise after...that?' He waved his arm towards Felice and Danny.

'That...' Kate waved her arm in the same direction '...has nothing to do with the original issue.'

He stared at her as if she'd gone mad. Like he had that first day on the beach. But she'd succeeded in getting him to loosen up then, hadn't she?

'Okay, it has everything to do with it,' she amended. 'It's a result of the original issue. But do you want these results to continue? Felice will eventually have children. There'll be christenings and events.' Did he want to be excluded from those?

Was he so angry he'd exclude himself for ever?

He gripped her shoulders and anguish blazed in the depths of his eyes, quickly masked. He'd lost Felice. She could see that knowledge burning there. He'd lost her for ever because, even if he healed the breach, Felice lived here now—ten thousand miles away.

Kate's vision blurred. She had so much—Jesse, Danny and Felice, the extended family of Archie and her crew. Simon had nothing. No one. And he deserved everything.

'Do what you came here to do, Simon,' she croaked. There was no other way forward.

'What…what is Kate talking about?' Felice whispered to Simon. She'd pulled both of Danny's arms around her in a kind of protective shield and leaned back against his chest. As always, Danny took everything in but said nothing.

Simon released Kate's shoulders and turned to Felice. Slowly. As if he was weary. As if he was a hundred years old.

'I waited for you, Felice, because I wanted to apologise.'

Felice moistened her lips. 'Apologise?'

'For being such a boor and a bully; for trying to control your life. I had no right to, but all I could see were the pitfalls, the ways you could be hurt.'

'You didn't trust me.'

'No, and it was wrong of me, and I am sorry.' His lips twisted briefly. 'I was hoping we could start again, but it seems you've forged a new life for yourself.' He nodded to Danny and then Felice. 'As I said before, I wish you both happiness.' Then he turned, walked out of the door and strode away.

'Kate?' Felice whispered, stricken.

'Think, Felice, think!' Kate had a sudden urge to shake the younger girl. 'Simon told me a little about your childhood and how your parents were rarely there.' Couldn't Felice see what she'd done?

Felice searched Kate's face, her eyes intent. Danny said, 'Steady on, Kate,' but both women ignored him.

'How much did you love him when you were little, how important was he to you?'

'He was…everything.'

'And how much do you think he loves you? How important do you think you are to him?'

Felice dashed away a tear. 'But he told me I was irresponsible, rash…that I'd disgrace him and myself.'

'Oh, Felice, why do you think he said those things? Can't you see he'd do anything—descend to blackmail, threats, anything—to keep you from harm? He knows now how wrong that was.'

'So why did he leave like…that?' She waved at the now empty doorway.

'Because you excluded him from sharing what should've been one of the happiest days of your life. Think of the way your parents treated him, the way they treated you.' She pulled in a breath. 'Felice, can't you see that you've just treated him the same way they always did? In a very vital way, you've just told him he's not important to you.'

Felice covered her mouth with both hands, her eyes wide with horror—silently begging Kate to tell her what to do to make things right.

'I think,' Kate started gently, 'that you need to make him unthink that as soon as possible.'

Felice shot out of the door before Kate had even finished her sentence.

The air whistled out between Danny's teeth. 'You could've gone a bit easier on her, couldn't you?'

She folded her arms. 'I think you and Felice have had things too easy for far too long as it is. I'm sorry, Danny, but the honeymoon's over. Sit. There are things we need to discuss.'

Simon and Felice were gone for nearly two hours. In their absence, Kate and Danny tossed a salad and prepared steaks for the barbecue.

There was work to be done and tonight she didn't need distractions.

When Simon and Felice finally walked through the back door, Felice sent Kate a relieved smile before rushing into Danny's arms. Simon took in the arrangements for the meal and backed up. 'It's getting late. I should leave and let you eat.'

'We've prepared enough for you too,' Kate said, her stomach turning over at the sight of him.

He hesitated.

'I was hoping you'd stay and eat with us.'

He smiled then, his eyes warm as they rested on her face, making her breath catch. 'I'd like that.'

'Good. That's settled, then.' Lord, did that voice belong to her? She shot a quick glance at Danny and Felice but they were too caught up in each other to notice anything amiss. Thank heavens. Though their single-minded focus on each other, the in jokes and teasing, and the touching—so much touching!—cranked up the tension in Kate until her throat went dry and she thought she might have to groan out loud to stop herself from exploding.

She gulped. 'Simon and I will cook the steaks.' She sent him an apologetic smile. 'It seems I'm always putting you to work.'

'I don't mind.' His grin widened to pure wickedness. 'I like it when you find…uses for me.'

'And you two can set the table,' she squeaked as she seized the plate of steaks and beat a hasty retreat to the cool of the back garden.

'Where's Jesse?' Simon asked, following her outside.

'He's already in bed.' When Simon didn't say anything she added, 'He was tired and I thought it might be a good idea to have…adult time this evening.'

'You're a good mother, Kate. You wanted to shield him from any potential unpleasantness and tension.'

'I did,' she agreed. 'But I didn't want you and Felice, or Danny for that manner, constrained by his presence. There are times and places for things. This evening is for you and Felice.'

Felice stuck her head outside. 'Do you want to eat inside or out?'

'Inside,' Kate called back. Tonight she wanted to see everyone's face by electric light, not half hidden by the dark.

'Why in?' Simon asked, laying the first of the steaks on the hotplate. It sizzled and spat, but he didn't flinch.

She tried not to notice how lean and sure his fingers were as they lifted the second and then the third steaks from the plate she held. The plate grew lighter. And so did she. 'Oh, um…'

she tried to roll her eyes '…it'll give them at least five more minutes of privacy if they're in there and we're out here.'

His laugh rumbled out of him, low and full of promise. 'That means we have five more minutes of privacy too, doesn't it?'

Privacy?

He placed the last steak on the barbecue. She sighed. Such magical fingers. They'd been sure and skilful as they'd explored her stomach and ribs, the undersides of her breasts.

They didn't need privacy! She jerked away from him, shocked at the ferocity of need pounding through her. This couldn't work. They'd discussed it more than once. She wouldn't indulge in a fling—she was a mother with responsibilities. What if she fell pregnant? How would Simon cope? How would she cope?

And anything longer-term was out of the question.

She had a son. He didn't want children.

She lived in Dutchman's Bay. He lived in England.

Impossible. Utterly impossible.

So why couldn't she stop fantasizing about those lean fingers on her body and those firm lips on hers?

'I believe I owe you an apology.'

His words jerked her back to the present. 'I doubt that,' she managed. And if he said anything about the high colour burning in her cheeks, she'd blame the heat from the barbecue.

'I don't believe I behaved very well when I first found out Felice and Danny had married and I—'

She reached up, pressing her fingers against his mouth. 'Don't apologise. You felt betrayed by all of us. I'd have felt the same.'

He took her hand, pressing a kiss to its palm, and then released it as if he didn't trust himself to hold it any longer than that.

'I know now that Felice swore you to secrecy.'

Kate didn't say anything. His concern for her felt right all the way down to her bones. It should feel wrong. But, no matter how hard she tried, she couldn't make it feel wrong.

'I just want you to know that I don't hold you responsible

for anything Felice has done in the past or anything she will do in the future.'

'Thank you.' She gave up fighting the rightness. 'Now turn the steaks, Simon.' She handed him the tongs. If she didn't deflect his attention away from her, she'd be in danger of having to kiss him.

Dinner was fun. They toasted each other—with beer, because they'd forgotten to chill the champagne. Felice rattled on non-stop about the sights she'd seen on her honeymoon—the beaches and reefs, the fabulous snorkelling and surfing. When her chatter finally petered out, Kate kicked Danny's shin beneath the table.

He dropped his fork and glared at her before turning his attention to Simon. 'Kate tells me you've plans to turn Holm House into a wedding and convention centre.'

'That's right.'

'It sounds exciting.'

Kate listened—and watched—carefully as Danny shot question after question at Simon. Her brother had a degree in business management. Beneath all that shaggy blond hair, he had a good head for business.

She'd miss it.

She kicked him again.

His teeth clenched as if he were biting back a retort and Kate had to choke back a laugh. Obediently, he turned to Felice. 'You know what, Flick—?' he used his pet name for her '—this venture of Simon's is really something. Big. I could be talking out of turn here, but…it's your family home too, isn't it? And maybe we should…you know?' He finished on a less than elegant shrug.

Kate didn't bother to berate him about that. From the way Simon stiffened beside her and Felice's jaw dropped, they had both certainly caught his drift.

Way to go, Danny! She wanted to high-five him.

'But…but what about Kate and *The Merry Dolphin*?' Felice finally managed to say.

Danny snorted. 'Believe me, Kate could run six boats, bring up ten kids, all while juggling three chain-saws if she wanted.'

Did he really think so? She beamed at him. This was going exactly to plan. 'Just the one boat will do.' She had no plans to expand. Not now.

Felice stared at her, then at Danny in dawning horror. 'But…you'd hate England, Danny. We only have one week of sunshine the whole year. Surf beaches are practically non-existent.'

'Pooh, Danny does too much surfing as it is.' Kate wound up for another kick.

As if he sensed that, Danny quickly added, 'I could never hate a fellow cricket-playing nation, Flick. And it's where you come from. I'd love to see it.'

'Then we'll visit. Of course we'll visit.'

'But this project of Simon's…it's seriously exciting. And it'll take longer than a visit to organise a wedding, won't it? Even if Holm House is in the process of gearing up for that kind of thing.'

'Wedding?' Felice said faintly.

'Too right,' Danny said.

He swallowed and if Kate had any doubts before about how much her brother loved Felice she certainly didn't now.

'We'll have to renew our vows in front of all your family and friends. We'd want to put on a nice do for everyone. And you'd get to do the whole white dress thing and…everything.'

From the corner of her eye, Kate could've sworn she saw Simon shake his head at Felice.

'I didn't come to Australia just to get away from Simon, you know, Danny. I…I'm a lady and there're all these constraints and expectations of me when I'm in England. I hate it. I don't want to go back.'

Danny glanced at Kate with a mixture of defeat and panic…and a tiny bit of relief.

'Running away isn't the answer,' Kate said in her most

bracing tone. She had to find something to say that would convince Felice to return to England. 'If you hate the constraints so much, challenge them, change the way things are done, blaze a trail and pull tradition into the twenty-first century.'

Felice stared at her as if she'd grown two heads. It reminded her of the way Simon looked at her sometimes and she wondered if she'd overdone it.

And then she saw Simon kick Felice beneath the table!

Kate gaped at him. 'I saw that!'

'What? You think you're the one who has the monopoly on kicking people beneath the table?' he demanded. 'You've kicked Danny twice already. If you don't stop soon he'll be black and blue.'

'No, I haven't.' She gulped and lifted her chin. Her face started to burn.

Danny started to laugh. 'You are such a bad liar, sis.'

'I'm just—'

'Trying to make things right for everyone,' Simon said. 'Like you always do.'

She slumped back in her seat. She brightened a moment later. 'Danny and Felice, you guys could work part of the year here and part of the year in England. You could have two summers each year. How cool's that?'

Simon threw his head back and laughed. 'Kate, butt out.'

Her jaw dropped. He reached across and tapped it closed— with those sure, tanned fingers that could send a girl's blood rushing through her ears.

'I know what you're doing.' He smiled and it warmed her to her very toes. 'And I appreciate it. But Felice and Danny have to make their own decisions now.'

She opened her mouth, but he cut in before she could speak. 'Without pressure from you...or me.'

She knew he was right. But it didn't mean she wanted him to return to England on his own. She kicked a table leg. 'Fine,' she muttered. 'No butting in.'

'So there you have it.' Simon spread his hands wide, his smile just as wide, as he addressed Danny and Felice. 'You can stay here and continue working on *The Merry Dolphin*, you can come and work on the estate with me, you can flit between the two, or you might decide to become ski instructors in Switzerland. Your call.'

Felice's eyes nearly popped out of her head. Kate couldn't resist winking at her. Something in the way Simon had just said all that, the lack of tension in his body, told her he would be okay with whatever choice Danny and Felice made. And Kate suddenly realised that was all she cared about.

Felice and Danny disappeared the moment the dishes were done with the excuse that they had a lot to discuss. From the way Simon's lips twitched, Kate knew he'd come to the same conclusion she had.

He lifted his mug. 'Let's take these outside.'

Kate hadn't really wanted coffee, but she hadn't wanted Simon to leave yet either. She'd offered coffee. He'd accepted.

She followed him outside although she knew she should call him back, tell him that if he wanted to talk they'd best do that at the kitchen table by the unromantic glow of the electric light. Alone with Simon in her garden in the dancing silver moonlight? They'd done this before. It had led to pulse-jumping kisses, soul-drugging kisses. She set her shoulders, lifted her chin. As long as she wrapped a good thick coat of common sense about herself while they were out here, then maybe she'd...

He turned. His eyes blazed. Kate trembled and all sense fled.

'I came racing up here this afternoon to tell you something.'

She remembered the look that had blazed across his face then too. She trembled again.

He set his coffee down on the table. He reached out and took her mug and set it down beside his. Then he drew her into his arms. She couldn't stop from lifting her face to his. Her pulse galloped, her breathing grew uncertain and, although she willed her bones to stay strong, they started to melt into him.

Sadness flashed through her. 'Don't kiss me, Simon.' She pushed a hand against his chest to push him away, but the moment she registered the steady thud of his heart against her palm it melted into him too.

She closed her eyes and took a breath.

'Kate?'

'You said you wouldn't hurt me or mine.' The words left her on a sob. Why hadn't she stayed in the house? To put themselves through this kind of torture would help no one.

His hands came up to cup her face. 'Never,' he vowed vehemently, his voice reverberating in the dark. 'I would never do anything to hurt you.'

Then let me go! But the words wouldn't come and, although she ordered them to, her legs refused to step away.

'Kate, I—'

'Mummy?'

Simon stiffened. Kate blinked. Then she wrenched herself out of Simon's arms. 'Jesse, baby? Where are you?'

'Here.'

His voice wobbled and it tore at her heart. She sensed rather than saw his solid shadow. She opened her arms and he ran straight into them. She brushed the hair off his forehead and held him tight. 'What's up, chook? Why aren't you asleep?'

'I had a dream that the Indians came and took me, and you couldn't find me even though I called really, really loud. They had big spears and bows and arrows. I had to come and find you.'

'Shh, of course you did. But it was just a dream, chook. And I'm here now.'

He nodded and started to relax against her. 'Can I sleep in your bed with you tonight?'

It had been a long time since he'd asked if he could do that. She hesitated before nodding. 'Okay then, just this once.' Had he picked up on her tension, her heartache? She closed her eyes and gulped. Jesse was her priority. She had to do everything she could to make his world secure.

She opened her eyes and met Simon's silver gaze. 'It's getting late,' she murmured.

He glanced down at his hands. 'I do need to talk to you.'

Her resolve faltered for a moment. 'Not tonight,' she forced herself to say. The night was too dangerous.

'Tomorrow?'

'I'm piloting *The Merry Dolphin* tomorrow.' Archie had the day off. 'The first tour is at ten if you'd like to tag along.'

'I'll see you then.' He nodded. 'Goodnight, Kate. Goodnight, Jesse.' Then he disappeared into the night.

Simon arrived at *The Merry Dolphin* half an hour before the first scheduled tour, but he still didn't get Kate alone. Pete was already aboard, buffing and shining.

'Need a hand?' Simon didn't have much experience at buffing and shining, but he'd buff and shine Kate's boat till it gleamed if it'd earn him a smile.

Not that one had to earn Kate's smiles—she gave them away for free.

'Nah, mate, sit down and tell me why England isn't doing so crash hot in their one-day series.'

Simon couldn't help grinning. England and Australia weren't playing each other this summer, thank goodness, but it didn't seem to stop the cricket enthusiasts from pointing out his team's current poor form…and ribbing him about it.

Kate rescued him less than five minutes later, leaping on board. 'Simon, this is Lionel, another member of our crew. Lionel, Simon is—'

'Probably stuck with tea and coffee making duties again,' he said on a mock sigh, shaking Lionel's hand.

Kate handed around takeaway cappuccinos and a bag of doughnuts, seized a clipboard from behind the bar. 'Okay, the itinerary today…'

Simon watched and listened and his heart billowed in pride at her strength and professionalism. Things couldn't have been easy for her when Jesse had come along, especially with her father gone. But she'd made something good of her life.

Something very good. He glanced around the bay. Everywhere he looked he saw sparkling water, golden sand and pretty beachside villages. Doubt slammed into him then. How could he compete with—

'Simon?'

Kate's hand on his arm hauled him back. She hitched her head upwards. 'Would you like to join me?'

'Yes.' Absolutely and utterly.

'Now, there was something you wanted to talk to me about?'

They were seated on the upper deck—alone—and all around him the bay gleamed and sparkled. Did the sun ever stop shining here? The blonde of her hair gleamed and the blue of her eyes sparkled. She looked as right here as the beaches and the dolphins and the gum trees that grew right to the water's edge in some places.

This was her home.

And what he wanted from her...

He couldn't just blurt it out. Not here. Not like this. Not at the beginning of her working day. What the hell was he thinking?

No, he had to do this right.

'Kate?' Pete's head appeared at the top of the stairs. 'Can we fit a group of fifteen senior citizens on the second tour?'

Kate glanced at her clipboard, ran a finger down the page and nodded. 'Yes, but make sure you still get a name and contact number.'

Pete waved and disappeared.

'That lot'll keep you busy with tea and coffee, let me tell you.' Then she blinked and her cheeks turned pink. 'I mean, if you're hanging around that long, that is.' She buried her nose in her paper cup and refused to look at him.

A grin burst through him. And hope. 'I'm hanging around all day.'

She met his gaze then, giving him one of those smiles he'd pay a million pounds for. 'So? What did you want to talk to me about?'

He couldn't help himself. He leaned forward and brushed his lips across her temple. She smelt of fresh cotton and coconut-scented sunscreen. He pulled back before he could nibble her ear, her neck…her lips. 'I think it can wait till later.'

He would do this right.

'If you're sure…'

He was sure. He wasn't going to risk interruptions. When he asked Kate to marry him, he wanted her full attention.

CHAPTER NINE

Simon spent the day helping out behind the bar, making tea and coffee and watching Kate. Her enthusiasm and passion for her job, for the dolphins, for the conservation of the bay, fascinated him.

Who was he trying to kid? Everything about her fascinated him.

And it appeared he wasn't the only one. She had a natural warmth that drew people to her. On each of the day's three tours the passengers on the upper deck gathered around her, firing questions at her, and she answered them with an ease born both of practice and a natural intelligence.

He listened and watched and his admiration grew. She wasn't just good at her job. She was brilliant. He could see her at Holm House, taking groups of visitors around and revealing historical titbits about the house, charming everyone with her smile and zest.

Hope powered through him. He tried to stamp down on his rising tide of impatience and when he turned to look at her he found it wasn't that hard. No day spent in the sun with Kate could be deemed wasted. No day in the rain either, for that matter. But it didn't stop him from aching for that afternoon walk along the foreshore when the shadows would start to lengthen and the breeze would drop…and they'd be alone.

'Did you enjoy the day?' Kate let Simon take her hand and help her from the boat and down to the pier. She shouldn't need help, but talking to Simon and looking at him, at the same time as walking…well, that just seemed beyond her today.

He smiled that holiday-maker smile—the one that made her want to do back flips. The smile that made her believe, contrary to all evidence otherwise, that she could walk on her hands.

'I had a great day.'

If anything, the intensity of his smile increased. Her tongue refused to trip off a single word in response. She feared if she opened her mouth now all that would emerge would be half-strangled words and drool. Such a bad look. She forced her eyes to the front and concentrated on placing one foot in front of the other. She stumbled when he took her hand.

'Steady.'

His voice sounded close by her ear and his breath brushed tendrils of her hair against her neck and cheek. What on earth…? She couldn't look at him, she couldn't talk, but she didn't pull her hand away. She did all she could to remain upright.

An ache stretched through her. All day Simon had laughed and joked—with her, with Pete and Lionel, with the passengers. Yet it had felt as if each and every smile had been for her alone. He'd gone and done that stupid thing and made her feel like a princess.

And she knew where thinking like that would get her.

Unless…

Simon had been in the oddest mood all day—a strange mixture of contentment and excitement. Hope arrowed straight to her heart, lifting her. What if he'd found some way to stay here in Nelson's Bay?

No, no. She kept placing one foot in front of the other. He'd told her he was tied to England for at least ten years. Her steps faltered. She tried to shake the notion away, but her hope wouldn't budge.

What if he'd found a solution?

Kate slammed to a halt and swung to him. She had to ask.

Now. But, as she opened her mouth, her mobile phone rang. With a grimace and a shrug, she flipped it open. 'Hello?'

'Where are you guys?'

Felice, she mouthed to Simon. 'On our way home,' she said to Felice.

Could it truly become Simon's home too? She crossed her fingers, and her toes. In another three weeks his hair would be the perfect length for running her fingers through.

'Have you passed the fish shop yet?'

She blinked, forced herself to glance about and take in her surroundings. 'Not yet.'

'What about prawns for dinner? I'll toss a salad, slice some fruit and…'

'Sounds wonderful. We'll grab some prawns on our way past.'

'Great! Can I speak to Simon?'

She handed him the phone. 'Game of cricket?' he said. 'Sure.' Then he handed the phone back to her with a twist of his lips. 'They're all in the park and they're going to walk around to meet us.'

She stared at those twisted lips, sensed his disgruntlement, and her hope shrivelled. What had she been thinking? 'You don't have to play with them if you don't want to.' Nobody was demanding he take time out for Jesse. In fact, she'd told him to pull back, hadn't she?

'It's not that.' He took her hand again. 'It's just…it's damn hard finding a moment alone with you. It could drive a man insane!'

Hope flailed back to life. 'We're alone now.'

'Not for much longer.' He pointed towards Dutchman's Bay. She could make out the figures of Jesse, Danny and Felice moving slowly but inexorably along the path towards them. 'And when I do finally get you alone, Kate Petherbridge, and say what I want to say, I want to make sure there won't be any interruptions.'

His glance seared her, heating her blood in a microsecond.

'And I want your full attention while I say it.'

She gulped and nodded. Oh, yes, he could be assured he'd have that.

How Kate made it through a rowdy game of beach cricket, the preparations for dinner and Danny and Felice's endless chatter—and touching!—she'd never know.

Nobody seemed to notice her distraction, though. Except Simon. His cool grey eyes saw too much, but she sensed his impatience too, his excitement.

For one awful moment, when all the dishes were cleared and Jesse put to bed, she thought Felice and Danny meant to hang around, share another bottle of wine and talk until the wee small hours.

No. No. No.

Across the table, her gaze met Simon's and suddenly she wanted to laugh. His lips twitched upwards too and all of her impatience eased from her. When the time was right, she and this man would talk.

And she had a feeling that this talk would be the most important of all her twenty-eight years, because one thing had become startlingly and amazingly clear. She loved Simon Morton-Blake with every atom of her being.

If he'd found a way to meet his obligations in England whilst staying here, she'd make sure he'd never regret it.

'Goodnight.' Simon's blood pumped with resolve as he watched Danny and Felice disappear around the side of the house for their flat above the garage. Without further ado, he stood and made for the chair beside Kate.

Once he was seated, she slipped her hand inside his as if it was the most natural thing in the world. He understood because that was exactly what it felt like.

'I love you.'

He hadn't meant to blurt it out like that. He'd meant to

build up to it. He hadn't expected the words to slip out so easily, so naturally.

'I know. I love you too.'

She spoke simply, like he had. Her delicious lips curved upwards and the tenderness in her smile humbled him. He wanted to sweep her up in his arms, but he knew it wouldn't stop at one kiss, and there was still so much to say. He contented himself with a grin—a grin he knew must take over his whole face.

Her grin matched it. Moonlight glinted off her hair, stars danced in her eyes. 'You are so beautiful.' *And she loved him.* He wanted to jump up and down, sing and dance and laugh, but that would mean letting go of her hand and he wasn't prepared to do that just yet.

'I think you're beautiful too.'

Her shy words caught at him, snagged at his chest, stealing his breath. He kissed her hand. 'I never believed in love at first sight.' What a fool he'd been. 'And then I clapped eyes on you.'

She leaned towards him, her eyes wide. 'Really?'

He grinned at the memory. 'You turned around from your filing cabinet on that Friday, your eyes widened…and I fell into them. I haven't stopped falling yet.'

'It was the moment after for me.' She reached out and touched the corner of his mouth. 'When you smiled. Nothing has been the same since.'

He turned to face her more fully. 'I was such a blockhead. With Jesse…' Regret fired through him. 'For so long I thought… But you changed all that.' He couldn't seem to complete a sentence, but her smile told him she followed his every thought without trouble.

Like she would for the rest of his life, he realised. This wonderful, remarkable woman was the other half of him. With her, he would never be alone again.

'I love Jesse now. You know that, don't you?' He had to make sure she knew that, felt the rightness of it.

'Yes.'

He reached out and cupped her face. She leant into it, her eyes filled with the same wonder that gripped him. *She loved him.* He wanted to shout it to the skies, only it would shatter the spell that surrounded them and he didn't want anything to break that. Not yet. 'You have given me such a gift,' he murmured.

She smiled. 'You're not afraid of fatherhood any more?'

'No. In fact, I am very much looking forward to learning all I can about fatherhood.' Starting with making those babies with this woman. An image of her pregnant with his child rocked him. A fierce longing seized him. He wanted that with this woman. He wanted it all with this woman.

'You'll make a wonderful father, Simon.'

'When you told me off yesterday—about messing with Jesse's feelings...'

She shifted on her chair and opened her mouth, but he pressed a finger to her lips. They trembled beneath it and desire burst to life, low and insistent, in his gut, but he wouldn't kiss her. Not yet. Things still needed to be said. 'It was only then that I realised how much I loved Jesse. I wanted to protect him...and you. It was the moment I realised I could be a good father—to Jesse and to whoever else might come along.'

A gleam lit her eyes. 'I would love to have your babies.'

Her voice came out low and husky. Possessiveness gripped him. 'You and me, we belong together, Kate.' She was his. And he was hers. 'I love you.' He gripped both her hands in his. 'Come to England with me—you and Jesse. Build a new life with me there. For ever.'

For a moment her whole face glowed, but then the gleam in her eyes started to dim, the space between her eyes crinkled in adorable puzzlement. He wanted to kiss it away, soothe it.

'But...' She gulped. 'But haven't you found a way to stay here in Australia?'

Regret shifted through him. He was asking her to give up so much—her home, her family—but they would build a new home. He would do whatever he could to give her the home she dreamed of, a home she could love.

'I can't stay here, Kate. I have too many obligations in England. But everything I have is yours. And we can come back here for holidays and visits.' He'd make sure they did that as often as possible.

She pulled her hands out of his. The crinkle between her eyes grew into a full-blown frown. 'I thought…'

Then the light went out in her eyes completely and fear fired his heart.

'I'm sorry, Simon. I can't go to England with you.'

He shot back in his seat. No! She couldn't mean that. She'd said she loved him.

She'd said she loved him!

'We belong together!' His words rang around the garden but he couldn't hold them back. The desolation in her eyes matched his. He swallowed and tried another tack. 'England isn't that bad, Kate. I mean, the weather isn't as good but…and I'm sure that between them Danny, Felice and Archie can keep *The Merry Dolphin* running, if you're worried about that and—'

'None of that matters!' She slashed a hand through the air. 'Merry Dolphin Tours can practically run itself, and I don't care about the weather.'

She reached out as if to touch him, but pulled back at the last minute as if she didn't trust herself. Her face twisted and he had to bite back an oath at her evident pain.

She gripped her hands together in her lap. 'Jesse,' she croaked out.

He wanted to fall down on his knees at her feet. 'But I swear to you—'

'It's not that!' Again she reached out towards him, and again she didn't touch him. 'I know you will make a great father. I don't doubt that.' Her eyes softened. 'I don't doubt you.'

'Then what?' he burst out. He leapt out of his chair and

started to pace, trying to control the rage and pain that threatened to overtake him. Not rage at her, but at whatever it was that held her back, at himself for not making this easier for her.

She covered her eyes. Her hand trembled before she pulled it away again. He fell back into his chair and managed to stop himself from dragging her into his arms—just—from trying to ease her obvious distress. If he did, he had a feeling she would cry, and she was holding herself together so tightly he instinctively knew that she wouldn't thank him for breaking that control.

'Just because you've come to know Jesse, to love him, doesn't mean you can replace his father. Simon, Jesse already has a dad. A good one.'

Paul! He reared back as if slapped.

'And that dad lives here in Nelson's Bay. It would not be fair to uproot Jesse if it means he loses his father. I...I couldn't do that to Jesse or Paul. They adore each other,' she finished on a whisper.

She was right.

Kate was one hundred per cent right. As always. The knowledge slammed into him, his newfound clarity sickened him, but he refused to look the other way. He'd become so caught up in his fantasy of him, her and Jesse together for ever that he hadn't let reality intrude.

And that was all it was, all it had ever been—a fantasy. A rock settled in his chest where his heart had once been.

'I'm sorry, Simon. So very, very sorry.'

So was he.

He roused himself. Took both her hands in his. 'You have nothing to apologise for. You love your son. You want what is best for him. You are a good mother. It's one of the things I love about you.'

'Thank you.'

Her eyes shimmered. The pain in them tore at him. He should've let her be. Like he'd always meant to. But he couldn't find it in his heart to regret loving her. She'd given him so much.

And yet he'd given her nothing in return. He'd never forgive himself for hurting her. A chill chased away all his former warmth, all his anticipation. Very slowly, he released her hands, easing himself away from her. 'Goodnight, Kate.'

He rose and strode off into the dark. He left her garden and didn't look back.

Kate watched Simon disappear into the shadows—his back stiff, his shoulders hunched, his strides long. She pressed the heel of her hand to her mouth to stifle a sob.

She would not cry. She would not.

But when she closed her eyes, all she could see was the devastation in Simon's face.

'Mum!'

Jesse? She half turned, but stopped herself in time. She didn't want him to see the poor job she'd done at not crying. It would frighten him.

Small arms were flung around her neck. 'Don't cry, Mummy. Please don't cry,' he sobbed against her neck.

She gulped her sobs back and huddled him close, but she couldn't stem the tears that coursed down her cheeks. She dragged him onto her lap and tucked his head beneath her chin so he couldn't see them. 'What's up, chook?'

'Simon is going away, isn't he?'

'He has to.'

'But I don't want him to. Not if it makes you sad.'

She raised her face to the sky and forced her eyes wide to stem the tears. She prayed the breeze would dry all traces of them from her cheeks. 'Remember how I told you it's okay to cry when you're sad?'

He nodded.

'Well, that goes for grown-ups too.'

'I don't want you to be sad,' he whispered.

Of course he didn't. He loved her with a completeness that sometimes awed her. Her heart might be breaking, but as she held him close she knew she'd done the right thing. She'd known the heartbreak of growing up without one of her parents. She would not let that be Jesse's fate.

'Well, now—' she pursed her lips and forced the beginnings of a smile, adjusting him in her lap so he could see her face '—no one can be happy a hundred per cent of the time.' She made herself grin. 'So I'll just have to settle for ninety-nine per cent of the time instead. And this has just been my itsy-bitsy one per cent.'

He stared at her, his eyes wide.

'See?' She smiled and kissed him on the nose to make him smile too. 'I'm going to be A-OK.'

'You promise?'

'I promise.'

'Do you want me to sleep with you tonight?'

She pretended to consider it. 'No, I think I will be fine, thank you. Besides—' she tickled him '—you'd keep me awake all night with your snoring.'

He wriggled under her searching fingers. 'I don't snore.' He giggled.

'C'mon.' She set him on the ground. 'It's time you were tucked up in bed.'

She took his hand and led him back into the house.

When Kate woke the next morning, she found Jesse's head on the pillow beside her and his eyes regarding her steadily.

'Good morning, chook. How long have you been here?'

'For a bit.'

It couldn't have been for too long. She hadn't fallen asleep until the wee small hours and a glance at the clock told her it wasn't much past six now.

'And I was very, very careful not to snore.'

'I greatly appreciate your thoughtfulness.'

Jesse didn't giggle like he normally would. 'Are you still sad?'

She gave a mock glare. 'Do I look sad to you?'

Jesse didn't answer and she thought perhaps it might be better not to have asked that question. She brushed the hair out of his eyes. 'What's on for school today? Sport?'

'Couldn't we make Simon stay?'

Oh, dear. She tried to pull a silly face. 'Ooh, like lock him up in the dungeon?'

He gave her one of those looks. 'We don't have a dungeon, Mum.'

'The attic, then?'

'We don't have one of those either. But—'

She pressed a finger to his lips. 'Simon can't stay, sweetheart, even though he wants to. He's in charge of a big, big house and—'

'How big?'

'It could be as big as our whole street for all I know.'

'That big,' he breathed. 'Wow.'

'I know.' She jumped out of bed. 'Let's look it up on the computer.'

She let Jesse fire up the computer whilst she made coffee. 'What do I type in?' he asked.

'Try Holm House.' She squeezed into the seat beside him and spelt it out for him. She sipped her coffee as the computer chugged away for a bit…

Both their jaws dropped at the same moment. The most impressive house Kate had ever seen outside of a period drama appeared on screen—huge, regal…had she already thought *huge*?

Jesse turned to her, all eyes. '*That's* where Simon lives?'

She gulped, running her finger along the accompanying blurb. 'Uh-huh, the residence of the seventh Lord of Holm—that's Simon. Has been used in movie sets and…and…'

'Wow!' Jesse stared at her, then back at the screen. 'Wow!'

'Yep.' She nodded. 'Wow. You see, Jesse, it's a very important house because of…' she floundered for a moment

'…because of history. Kings and queens have stayed there.' Now she was just making it up as she went along, but England had had a lot of kings and queens. Surely one of them had stayed on the Holm estate. 'And it's Simon's job to look after that house. He's promised to preserve it for…for future generations. He's going to let people have their weddings and conferences there, and make films…and stuff,' she finished lamely.

Her eyes started to burn. Had Simon really wanted to share all of this with her?

She snapped to when she realised Jesse was watching her with big grave eyes. 'And that's why Simon has to go back to England,' she said.

Jesse sighed. 'I bet having a house like that means he's awful busy.'

'I bet you're right. But you know what else? I bet Simon would love to have you as his email buddy.'

He brightened. 'You think so?'

'I'm sure of it.'

Jesse and Simon had formed a bond. Time and distance might weaken it, perhaps even destroy it, but she wouldn't. No sirree.

'C'mon, mister. Let's make pancakes for breakfast and then it's off to school with you.'

And no more daydreaming for her.

'Pop the champagne, Danny,' Felice ordered, striding outside and setting an enormous pan of paella, bursting with plump prawns and juicy mussels, onto the table.

It looked heavenly, and probably smelt heavenly, and if Kate could draw a proper breath perhaps she'd manage to appreciate it more.

Felice beamed around the table. 'We're going to toast Simon's last night—on this visit, at least—in style.'

Simon's last night. Here. In Australia.

If her eyes didn't keep clouding over perhaps she'd appreciate the beautiful table setting Felice had arranged with so much care too—a pretty tablecloth, frangipani flowers floating in a bowl of water, crystal champagne flutes. French champagne.

Kate sighed. She couldn't seem to dredge up an ounce of enthusiasm for any of it. Everything seemed deadened and dull. The champagne she sipped, the salt-drenched air, even the view spread out in front of her lacked colour and life.

'Hey!'

Jesse? That spun her around. 'What are you—'

Paul! She leapt to her feet. What was wrong? What had happened?

'We made it,' Jesse cried, dragging Paul to the table.

Of course. Kate sat. Felice wouldn't have forgotten to invite Jesse for Simon's last dinner. And Jesse wouldn't have missed it for the world.

Kate pasted on her happy face.

Felice doled out large servings of paella. Kate wanted to tell her not to make her serving too large, but she didn't want to sound ungracious. Her face started to ache from her happy smile. Beside her, she could sense Simon's tension. Sitting beside him, dragging in drugging breaths of his cool scent, was probably better than sitting across from him, ogling his superb shoulders in that navy polo shirt that darkened his eyes.

Because she knew it wasn't the shirt that darkened his eyes, but pain. And she couldn't reach out and wipe that pain away. So sitting beside him rather than opposite was infinitely preferable. For him too, she guessed. He wouldn't see her happy smile for the sham it was.

'I'm glad you could make it,' Felice said to Paul, handing him a laden plate.

'I had to come,' he said simply. 'Jesse is worried about Kate.'

The entire table stilled. Then, as one, turned to stare at Kate.

'Oh, Jesse.' But her son stared down at his plate and wouldn't meet her eyes.

Paul glared at Simon. 'He said you made her cry.'

'Can we talk about this in private?' she hissed at Paul.

He shook his head once—hard. 'We're all family here, Kate. We care about you.'

'But—'

'Let the man speak for himself.'

Kate slumped back. 'I'm sorry about this, Simon.'

Simon reached out and covered her hand with his. Warmth flooded through her. 'You have nothing to apologise for.' And then he removed his hand and the warmth drifted away and was gone.

Just like Simon would be gone. Tomorrow.

Simon straightened his shoulders. 'Jesse is right. I did make Kate cry. I didn't mean to.' He hauled in a breath. 'I've hurt her and I'll regret it to my dying day. I'm very sorry.'

Paul stared at Simon and then his shoulders sagged. 'You're in love with her.'

It was a statement, not a question, but Simon answered anyway. 'Yes.'

'And Mummy loves Simon.'

Felice dropped the serving spoon. It splattered the tablecloth and almost upset the bowl of frangipani flowers. She stared at Kate and Simon. 'I had no idea.' She sank into her chair, one hand covering her mouth.

No. She and Danny had been too caught up in their post-honeymoon bliss. As they should be. Kate didn't blame them for that. She didn't blame anyone.

'But this is perfect!' Felice practically bounced out of her seat. 'You guys were meant for each other.'

Kate didn't say anything, nor did Simon. He didn't move so much as a muscle. She couldn't move anything.

Danny rested his arms on the table, leaning across it towards her. 'If you love him, Kate, then... Look, Felice and I, we want to stay here and run Merry Dolphin Tours. You've done every-thing for so long, it's time I pulled my weight. With Archie's help, Felice and I can take over, and you'd be free to go with Simon. You're not tied here.'

From somewhere she managed to find a smile. 'I may not be, but Jesse is.'

Danny sat back, glanced at Paul, then swore softly under his breath. 'Hell, I wasn't thinking. Sorry, Kate, Paul, I…'

She wanted to tell him it was okay, that she knew he only wanted her to be happy, but the effort was beyond her for the moment.

Felice shook her head, glancing around the table wildly. 'No, that can't be it! Paul could visit. Jesse can come back for school holidays and—'

'No!' Kate hadn't meant to speak so loudly. She didn't mean for Felice's eyes to fill up with tears either, but this had to be settled. 'I wouldn't dream of letting Paul take Jesse out of the country to live, leaving me to see him only on brief visits and school holidays. So I won't do that to Paul either. I won't do that to Jesse.'

With all her heart she wanted to pack up and follow Simon tomorrow—even if it meant leaving her home and her family. Somehow, Simon had become her family. But she couldn't do it if it meant Jesse suffered. Jesse had to come first.

'Jesse needs both me and Paul.' She pulled in a breath. 'This is for the best.' She glanced around the table with her fiercest smile. 'Now, c'mon guys, this is supposed to be a celebratory dinner. Chop-chop, Felice.' She clapped her hands. 'Keep serving; I'm hungry and I prefer my paella lukewarm, not stone-cold.'

Felice leapt up to serve, Danny tried to tell a joke but it petered out before he got to the punchline. Jesse ran around the table to her. His bottom lip wobbled. 'But you're still going to be sad!'

'No, I won't, chook. I'll be as cheerful and happy as ever.'

He placed his hands on either side of her face. 'Your mouth smiles, but your eyes aren't sparkly any more.'

The table gave a collective gasp. The serving spoon clattered into the bowl of frangipani flowers. Kate was too shattered to speak.

Simon's strong hands descended to Jesse's shoulders and turned him around. He smiled at Kate over the top of Jesse's head—a buck up smile. She tried to buck up.

'Jesse—' he started in that to-die-for accent of his '—as long as your mum has you she'll never be truly sad. More than just about anything, she wants you to be happy, and I know you understand that because you want her to be happy too.'

Jesse nodded. 'Uh-huh.'

'But, even more than that, she wants what's best for you. It might make you happy to have a second bowl of ice cream or to eat a whole block of chocolate, but she's not going to let you do that because she knows it'll give you a stomach ache and rot your teeth. You might want to race outside without your hat and sunscreen, but she's not going to let you do that either because you might get sunburned.'

Jesse nodded again. ''Cause mums know what will make you sad later.'

Kate's soul filled with pride in her son.

'Your mum knows what's best for you,' Simon continued. 'And what's best is to have both her and your dad living nearby so you can see both of them whenever you want. Although it's hard and makes all of us a bit sad, what your mum is doing is right. Okay, mate?'

'Okay,' Jesse finally mumbled. Then he flung his arms around Simon's neck. 'But we'll miss you!'

Simon's strong arms went around her child and Kate couldn't suppress a sigh.

'I'll miss all of you too.' Slowly Simon drew back as if reluctant to release Jesse. 'But if it's okay with your mum and dad, maybe you could visit when Felice and Danny come over in June?'

'Wow, really?' Jesse swung to Kate, his eyes filled with hope. 'You could come too.'

She tried to smile, tried to make her eyes sparkly. 'Someone will need to stay here and pilot *The Merry Dolphin*.' She could not go to England and see Simon. She couldn't.

Jesse's face fell. 'But—'

She leaned forward, laying a finger against his lips. 'Enough for now, okay. We'll talk about it when the time gets closer. We're supposed to be making Simon's last night here fun. So back around the table and eat your dinner, young man.'

Felice, with tears pouring down her face, continued to serve out what Kate suspected was now stone-cold paella. All Kate wanted to do was rest her head against the table top and groan. Beneath the table, Simon gripped her hand.

Her spine straightened. She sent him a smile. With Simon beside her she'd find the strength to get through this meal. Somehow.

Kate breathed a sigh of relief when Paul decided it was time to take Jesse home to bed, when Danny and Felice said it was their bedtime too…when the forced jollity around the table finally came to an end.

When everyone tactfully left her and Simon alone.

She closed her eyes and stretched her arms back over her head. 'I swear I thought it was never going to come to an end,' she groaned.

Simon's low chuckle skittered across her bare skin, raising goose-bumps.

'I'd put up with that and a whole lot more just to have a few minutes alone with you.'

She'd miss his voice, his scent.

He reached out his hand and she placed her own in it. They sat there, hands clasped, aching.

She'd miss his touch.

'I'm sorry about Paul puffing up earlier.'

'Don't be. He was worried about you. And understandably concerned that you wanted to take Jesse out of the country.'

She turned her head. 'I...I couldn't do that, Simon.'

He met her gaze. 'I know.' His hand tightened about hers. His eyes told her he understood. 'I admire you for it.'

She blew a strand of hair off her face. 'But now everyone knows.' She'd have much preferred to keep her grief to herself. 'Danny and Felice will be watching me like hawks now.' And probably treating her like an invalid.

'I'm glad they know,' Simon said. 'They'll look after you.'

'I can look after myself!'

'I know, but it makes me feel better knowing they'll be looking out for you too.'

'Oh, Simon.' She turned to face him. 'Who'll look out for you?'

With his free hand, he brushed her hair from her face and back behind her ear. 'You're not to worry about me, Kate.'

How could she not?

And just how did one go about making one's eyes sparkly? She'd try and do that for him right now if she could.

Simon's thumb moved back and forth across her bottom lip. 'You've given me far more than...than the pain of missing you will take away.'

She seized his hand, unable to take too much of a touch that sparked a red-hot desire in her.

'You've taught me what's really important in life and I won't forget.'

'Promise me you'll take regular holidays.'

'I promise.'

'And that you'll stop and smell the coconut oil.'

'And the roses,' he promised, his eyes gentle.

She managed a smile then. 'And when the time is right, you will become a father.'

A spasm of pain crossed his face. His hands tightened about

hers and she welcomed the sudden bite of pain. 'I can't promise you that,' he said, his voice ragged.

She reached out, wiped the lines from his face and very gently placed her lips on his. Their lips clung—briefly, too briefly—then parted.

'You made me feel like a princess,' she whispered.

He seized her face in his hands. 'Come and visit Holm House,' he urged. 'When Felice and Danny come. Or whenever you like. I swear you'll be treated like royalty and we'll—'

'No.' She drew back, her heart burning in protest. 'I can't.' The hope died on Simon's face. She hated that too, but she couldn't help it. 'That would be too hard for both of us.' If she started to visit him, she'd never get over him. He wouldn't find a way to move forward either.

She'd never get over him anyway.

She pushed that thought away. She'd find a way to make her eyes sparkly again. She had to. For Jesse's sake.

Simon drew her to her feet. His lips descended to hers—firm, warm...full of unspoken things that made tears press against the backs of her eyes.

She wouldn't let them fall. She would not let that be his last memory of her.

'I love you,' she whispered when he drew back.

His fingers brushed her face—a butterfly touch. 'Goodbye, Kate.'

He turned and was gone, swallowed by the shadows of her garden and beyond. When she could hear him no more, Kate felt behind her for her chair. She eased herself down into it, hugged her knees to her chest and stared out into the night.

CHAPTER TEN

KATE turned her head the tiniest fraction, an action designed to expend the least amount of energy possible. The bedside clock showed it was nine o'clock.

Danny and Felice had arranged to pick Simon up from his hotel and drive him to the airport at nine o'clock.

The airport in Sydney.

His flight wasn't till four, but they'd all agreed on the wisdom of leaving in plenty of time.

In case of traffic delays.

So they could take their time.

Just because…

In seven more hours, Simon would be in the air and heading for the other side of the world.

To England.

Kate didn't haul herself out of bed; she didn't dress or make coffee. She didn't see the point. She didn't want to get up, she didn't want to get dressed and she didn't want coffee.

She wanted Simon.

She wouldn't sleep. She hadn't slept all night. She'd lain here and stared at the ceiling ever since Felice had tiptoed out into the garden at midnight and told her it was time to go to bed.

Garden…bed… It hadn't mattered then and it didn't matter now.

It had mattered to Felice. It would matter to Jesse. But Jesse was at his dad's for the next few days and she'd worry about happy faces and sparkly eyes when he returned.

She stared at the clock and watched the minutes tick over. Had Simon left Port Stephens yet? Had he asked Danny to drive down the main street of Nelson's Bay just so he could gaze one more time at the spot where they'd first kissed?

Or had they turned straight onto the road that led to Sydney and the airport?

Loud banging on her front door jolted Kate awake. The clock showed it was ten twenty-six. Against all expectations, she'd fallen asleep.

She stared at the clock and didn't move. Simon would be through Newcastle by now and on the freeway halfway to Sydney…

More knocking—loud and intrusive. She ignored it. Whoever it was would eventually give up and go away, leave her in peace.

'Kate!'

Paul's shout pierced her apathy. She jerked upright on the bed. Jesse! Had something happened to Jesse? And here she was, slouching around like a limp fish feeling sorry for herself. She shot off the bed, bolted down the hallway and flung the front door open. 'What is it?'

Jesse and Paul both stood there grinning at her, inordinately pleased with themselves about something. She clutched the door in relief, sagging against it for a moment. 'What are you guys doing here?'

'Mum!' Jesse stared at her, scandalised. 'You're still in your pyjamas.'

'It's Sunday. I'm not working.'

Paul grinned. 'Morning, Kate.'

Oh, God! They hadn't concocted some hideous cheer Kate up scheme, had they? She didn't think she could face a picnic or ice cream sundaes or…anything. She bit back a very rude word. Paul wouldn't do that to her, surely? He wasn't a total numbskull, even if it would take her quite some time to forgive him for showing up at dinner last night and outing her heartbreak to all and sundry.

'Can we come in?'

She shook herself, waving her arm down the hall. 'By all means.'

'We've got great news, Mum!'

'Great news, huh?' She led them down the hallway to the kitchen, pulled out a chair at the kitchen table and collapsed into it. Jesse hopped from one foot to the other and she did her best not to sigh. He had way too much energy for her today. Just watching him made her want to crawl back into bed and drag the covers over her head.

Happy face, she ordered.

Paul set about making coffee. Instant. Ugh. But she didn't protest. She didn't care.

'The best news in the world,' Jesse said, nodding vigorously.

Paul leaned against the kitchen bench, arms folded, legs crossed at the ankles and kept grinning at her as he waited for the kettle to boil.

'The best news, huh?' She tried to inject enthusiasm into her voice. She'd played this game before. She knew her role. 'Let me guess—you got tickets to the twenty-twenty cricket match in Sydney?'

Jesse shook his head. Paul's grin widened, if that were possible. 'Thank heavens,' she murmured under her breath, because she couldn't think of a single excuse that would get her out of attending that.

'Okay, then…the characters from *Sesame Street* are having a show in town?'

Jesse rolled his eyes. 'I'm too old for that now, Mum.'

Ooh, that's right.

He started bouncing again. 'What's the one thing you want most in the world?'

Simon.

But she couldn't have him. She wouldn't say his name out loud either. She couldn't. But she couldn't think of a single thing to say instead. Jesse glared at her expectantly. 'Um…' She moistened her lips and glanced across at Paul for help.

'Go on, tell her,' Paul said to Jesse, obviously taking pity on her.

Jesse lunged forward to grab her arm and pump it up and down. 'We can go to England to live, Mum. We can! Honest we can!'

She stared from Jesse to Paul. He leant his forearms on the breakfast bar, hands lightly clasped, and spoke directly to her. 'You and I have sacrificed a lot of opportunities over the years for Jesse. I haven't regretted a single one of them. I love our son.'

She nodded. 'I know.' And suddenly she knew that Paul planned to suggest what she'd never have the strength to offer— that Jesse live with her for six months of the year in England, and then with him in Australia for the other six. She couldn't do it. She would not live without her son for six months of every year.

Jesse beamed at her. Her heart stretched so tight she thought it might snap.

'You know that in the last few years I've taken on a certain amount of freelance work from overseas.'

She gazed at Paul blankly, shrugged, then nodded. 'Uh-huh.' Paul was a graphic designer—a good one.

'Well…since then I've been offered positions with several of Europe's leading design firms.'

It took a moment for his words to collide with her grey matter. She blinked when they did, and straightened. Her heart started to thump.

'Naturally I turned them down. I wasn't moving away from Jesse.'

The pounding increased. 'But?' It was near impossible to push that one little word out of a throat that had tightened with suspense. And hope.

'After Jesse and I left here last night, I emailed two of the London-based firms to see if their offers still stood.'

'And...?' Her ribs contracted so hard around her lungs she couldn't utter a word longer than a single syllable. Even then it came out on a gasp.

'Half an hour ago I heard back from my first choice.' He straightened, opening his arms wide. 'The offer still stands. They want me on board asap.'

Kate's jaw hit the floor. He wasn't a numbskull but an angel, a fairy godmother! She leapt up, then didn't know what to do. Jesse flung his arms around her waist so she hugged him.

He tilted his head back to grin at her, his whole face alight with excitement. 'Cool, huh?'

Oh, yes—very, very cool!

In the next instant, although she did her best to ignore it, cold hard reality set in, dousing her excitement as she forced herself to assess Paul's offer rationally. 'This is asking an awful lot of you, Paul.' Her shoulders sagged. It was asking too much. She didn't want to say the words, but she forced them out. 'I couldn't possibly accept this kind of sacrifice. I—'

'Sacrifice?' Paul snorted. 'Kate, this is the kind of job I've always dreamed about.'

He meant it? The excitement shining in his face matched Jesse's, belying any notion she might have that he was making a sacrifice.

He meant it!

He shrugged. 'It does mean longer commute times than we currently have with Jesse. I understand the Holm estate is an hour and a half from the centre of London. It won't be a two-minute dash up the road from house to house any more. But...'

'But?' she echoed, hardly able to take it all in.

'And,' he added, pointing a finger at her, 'I want a big say in where Jesse goes to school.'

'Of course, you always have thus far, haven't you?'

His face broke out into a grin. 'Then let's do it. Let's move halfway around the world.'

Kate suddenly realised exactly what it took to make her eyes sparkly again. She had a feeling all of her sparkled. She leant down until she was eye to eye with Jesse before she sparkled right off the Richter scale. 'Are you sure you want to move away from the bay, Jesse? There won't be much swimming or fishing in England.'

'Yes, there will. Felice told me about the indoor swimming pool and there's a stream and a dam with fish in them.'

There was? Jesse knew more about their prospective new home than she did.

'And there's a tree-house and lambs I'll be allowed to feed and Dad said he'd take me to a test match at Lords and that there'll be heaps and heaps of cricket teams for me to play in.'

Kate started to laugh—right down in her heart laughter. 'I take it that's a yes, then?'

'Yes!'

'Woo hoo!'

She and Jesse proceeded to perform a very noisy victory dance all through the kitchen. Until Kate snapped to.

She grabbed Paul's arm to check his wristwatch. 'We have to go. Now!' She started herding him and Jesse to the front door. 'Simon's plane leaves in less than five hours and we have to tell him!'

'Kate—' Paul stopped her before she could race out of the front door '—I am not taking you to the airport...'

Her face fell.

'...in your pyjamas,' he finished.

She looked down at herself, groaned and stamped a foot. She covered Jesse's ears. 'Bugger!'

'Mum!'

'Sorry.' Why hadn't she forced herself up, got changed, had coffee?

'I'll go get changed. Coffee—' she pushed Paul back

towards the kitchen '—go make. You—' she pointed at Jesse '—find travel mugs, a Thermos, anything.' Then she bolted for her bedroom.

Paul sent Kate a wry glance. 'That is not going to make the car go any faster, Kate.'

'Sorry.' She tried to make herself sit back in the seat, hands in her lap instead of pressing against the dashboard, but too much energy zinged through her for stillness. 'Can't you…like, do something?' she burst out.

'I'm open to suggestions.'

'Don't you know a short cut to the airport?' she demanded. Preferably one that didn't involve so much traffic.

In the next instant she shook her head. 'No, no. It's always a really bad idea to take a short cut to the airport.'

'It is. Now relax; we'll be there soon.'

Relax? How could she relax? First there'd been an accident on the freeway that had held them up for an hour, and now this endless traffic had them crawling at a snail's pace. What if Simon had already passed through customs and security? This mad dash would all be for nothing.

'Why don't you call Simon's mobile?'

She twisted her hands together. 'I…um…don't know his number.'

Paul glanced at her, his lips twitched and then he burst out laughing. 'You're prepared to move halfway around the world to be with the guy, but you don't know his cell number?'

'Something like that,' she mumbled.

'Try Danny or Felice's phones.'

She already had. 'Felice's is switched off and Danny isn't answering.' She suspected he'd left it at home.

She twisted around to glance at the back seat. Jesse stirred. His eyes opened and in the next instant he shot bolt upright. 'Are we there yet?'

She grinned at the way his face lit up. 'Close.'

'Very close,' Paul said, turning into the airport car park. 'We're here.'

'Oh, God!' Kate groaned. 'Hurry! Hurry! Car park there. Now!'

She pointed and Paul slid the car into the space. Kate practically fell out in her haste. She grabbed one of Jesse's hands. Paul grabbed the other. 'Now run!' she ordered.

She slid to a halt once they entered the airport proper. Good Lord, there were so many people. How on earth would she find Simon in this crush?

'Check-in,' Paul said. 'We'll try there first.' He pointed to her left and she set off again at speed.

'Kate!'

'Felice!' She slid to a halt again, dropping Jesse's hand to seize Felice's shoulders. 'Simon,' she croaked. 'Where?'

Felice's gaze swept over Kate from the top of her head to the tips of her toes, her eyes widened, and Kate could only imagine what a sight she made. 'What are you doing here?'

'No time.'

'Hey, sis.'

She ignored Danny and shook Felice. 'Where?'

Felice grabbed her hand and dragged her through the crowd. Kate didn't glance behind to see if Danny, Jesse and Paul followed. She knew they would.

'We left him at the check-in desk. He left it to the very last minute to check in too, dawdling over so many coffees I thought he'd turn into an espresso machine.'

'So he wouldn't have made it to customs yet?' she gasped.

'I don't think so.' Felice dragged Kate to a halt. 'We left him here.'

Kate released Felice to pace the length of the barrier, searching for the familiar dark head with its too-short hair and shoulders broad enough to carry the weight of the world. She had to bite her tongue to stop herself from calling his name. She suspected she was acting enough of a loony as it was.

Then she saw him. He stepped forward towards the counter, suitcase in one hand, documentation in the other and Kate's tongue stuck fast to the roof of her mouth.

He wore a suit. He had a briefcase tucked against his side. He looked every inch the lord and something shivered inside her as her confidence slipped. Surely a single mother with a rowdy child would be a liability to him, not—

'Simon!'

Felice's shrill scream rang around the entire check-in point, momentarily deafening Kate.

'Ow.' Kate glared at her and covered her nearest ear. When she turned back, though, she saw that Felice's shout had achieved its objective. Every head had swung around towards them.

Everybody's—including Simon's.

Oh, Lord. He blinked. She gulped and swallowed, mouthed, 'Hi,' gave a tiny wave, because she had to do something, however inadequate. She didn't know what else to say. Or do. After Felice's shout, the airport seemed suddenly and eerily quiet.

He shifted his weight to the balls of his feet. The check-in clerk snatched up his documentation. Tiredness swept across his face. 'So you've come to see me off after all,' he called out when she didn't add anything to her initial greeting.

He looked so unfamiliar, so impeccably correct in his suit. And tie. She'd grown so used to seeing him in board shorts and T-shirts, chinos and polo shirts, that she'd forgotten—Simon Morton-Blake was the seventh Lord of Holm. What on earth would the seventh Lord of Holm want with her?

Then he smiled and he was just Simon. The sun came out and she knew she was still his princess. She threw her head back and laughed for the sheer joy of it. She moved around the barrier until she was as close as she could be to him and the check-in desk, but still too many bodies separated them. She swooshed the people with her hands, glaring at them until they moved to one side or the other, or at least as far as the barriers would let them, giving her a clear line of sight to Simon.

'Simon—'

She didn't know if she wanted to laugh or cry.

'Simon, we can come to England to live—me and Jesse!' She shouted the words out in much the same fashion as Jesse had to her only hours ago.

Simon frowned. Kate wondered if her words had come out coherently or if they'd only made sense in her head.

He went to move towards her when the check-in clerk snapped, 'If you move away from the counter, sir, you will have to go to the back of the line!' She glanced at his documentation, scowled at his ticket. 'I wouldn't recommend that, sir. Not with the flight you're trying to catch.'

He hesitated, an endearing indecision flashing across his face. He pointed a trembling finger at Kate. 'Will you repeat what you just said?'

Her heart swelled with love for him. She understood his fear of allowing himself to hope, his fear he hadn't heard her right the first time.

'Paul has been offered a job in London.' She turned and found Paul and Jesse, Danny and Felice, forming a small group nearby. 'Paul, what's the name of the firm you'll be working for?'

'Inglewood and Baxters.'

She turned back to Simon and repeated it. 'You know them?'

He nodded. He stared at her and his shoulders stiffened, then went slack as if a truck had hit him, or a thunderbolt. 'They're good. One of the best design groups in the world.'

Her heart swelled even more as she saw he still hadn't comprehended her meaning. 'Paul has been offered his dream job and he has accepted it.' She pulled in a breath. 'Which means Jesse and I are moving to England.'

She stared at him. He stared back. She waited for comprehension to dawn in those clear grey eyes of his. 'I don't mean right now, of course. It'll take us a few weeks to organise everything. But soon…if that's what you still want,' she finished on a gulp, nerves assailing her all over again.

'You're going to come to England? To live?'

'Yes!' She shouted the word, her nerves suddenly at stretching point.

Simon dropped his briefcase, kicked his suitcase out of the way and strode away from the counter, knocking barriers every which way.

'Sir!' the check-in clerk called. 'Sir, your passport, your suitcase. Your ticket!'

'I'm not taking that flight,' he shot back over his shoulder, his eyes never leaving Kate's face.

People scattered out of his way, barriers kept falling and then he was down on his knee in front of her and she found her hands clasped in his.

'Kate, you are the love of my heart. I have been dying by slow degrees today in this God-forsaken place, knowing that every minute was a minute closer to leaving you behind. Please, Kate, please…do me the very great honour of consenting to be my wife?'

If possible, the airport became even more hushed as all within earshot turned and held a collective breath, but Kate wasn't aware of anyone else other than the man in front of her, down on bended knee. She dropped to her knees too. They were decidedly useless and wobbly knees after that declaration. Especially when Simon insisted on steaming her up with an expression of such utter intensity she doubted whether her legs would work ever again.

'Yes,' she whispered. 'Yes, please, Simon. I would very much love to be your wife.'

With a whoop, Simon dragged her to her feet and swung her around. Kate found herself in the centre of a victory dance with her family. And then she realised it wasn't just her and Simon, Jesse and Paul, Danny and Felice, cheering and dancing and wiping their eyes, but what appeared to be half the airport too.

Which reminded her where they were. 'Oh, Simon, you're going to miss your flight.'

'I am.'

He didn't seem the least put out by that fact.

'I shall have to return to England at some time over the next week—meetings I can't get out of, I'm afraid, and documents that need signing. But then I'm coming back here to take you and Jesse home.'

It sounded heavenly.

'It takes one month after the notice of intent to get married in Australia.'

She blinked. 'How do you know that?'

'I looked it up.' His eyes darkened. 'I want to marry you on the beach at the exact spot where we first kissed.'

Her mouth went dry at the promise in that marvellous voice of his. 'I...um...we'd better wear our swimsuits then, because from memory it was a bit wet.' Not good for a frilly dress. 'Make it the spot where we did back flips and you have yourself a deal.' She wanted the frilly dress.

She wanted Simon. For ever.

'Done.' He gripped her face in his hands. 'I love you, Kate Petherbridge.'

She stared at those divine lips, trying to shake herself out of the trance threatening to descend on her. 'I love you too, Simon Morton-Blake.' She meant to spend the rest of her life proving to him exactly how much.

'Can you, Jesse and Paul be ready in a month?'

She'd make sure they were. 'Yes.'

His hands traced her face; his thumb followed the curve of her bottom lip. 'Once we're married we are never going to be separated again,' he vowed.

She twined her arms around his neck. 'Amen,' she whispered against his mouth the moment before his lips claimed hers and she could finally melt into him.

When Simon lifted his head, heaven only knew how many seconds or minutes later, Kate grew aware of the applause, the cheering, the people—strangers—who called out their congratulations and good wishes. Heat mounted her cheeks but she was too happy to be embarrassed for long. In fact, it seemed as if the happiness surrounding her and Simon rippled outwards in ever increasing circles, engulfing everyone nearby in its glow too.

She glanced down when Jesse squeezed in between her and Simon. 'Cool, huh?' he said, grinning up at Simon.

'You bet,' Simon said, swinging him up into his arms.

'I think Mum will be happy again now,' Jesse whispered.

Simon pretended to consider her. 'Her eyes are decidedly sparkly,' he agreed.

Jesse curved one arm around Simon's neck, the other around Kate's. 'I think we're all going to be happy.'

'That's the plan, bucko,' Simon said with a grin. 'I plan to dedicate my whole life to making you and your mum happy.'

'And whoever else comes along?' Kate whispered, touching her forehead to his.

'And whoever else comes along,' he said, his eyes dark with promise.

Kate winked at Jesse. 'Cool, huh?'

Jesse beamed back. 'You bet.'

* * * * *

*Celebrate 60 years of pure reading pleasure
with Harlequin®!
Silhouette® Romantic Suspense is celebrating with the
glamour-filled, adrenaline-charged series
LOVE IN 60 SECONDS starting in April 2009.
Six stories that promise to bring the glitz of Las Vegas,
the danger of revenge, the mystery of a missing diamond,
family scandals and ripped-from-the-headlines intrigue. Get
your heart racing as love happens in sixty seconds!*

Enjoy a sneak peek of
USA TODAY bestselling author Marie Ferrarella's
THE HEIRESS'S 2-WEEK AFFAIR
Available April 2009
from Silhouette® Romantic Suspense.

Eight years ago Matt Shaffer had vanished out of Natalie Rothchild's life, leaving behind a one-line note tucked under a pillow that had grown cold: *I'm sorry, but this just isn't going to work.*

That was it. No explanation, no real indication of remorse. The note had been as clinical and compassionless as an eviction notice, which, in effect, it had been, Natalie thought as she navigated through the morning traffic. Matt had written the note to evict her from his life.

She'd spent the next two weeks crying, breaking down without warning as she walked down the street, or as she sat staring at a meal she couldn't bring herself to eat.

Candace, she remembered with a bittersweet pang, had tried to get her to go clubbing in order to get her to forget about Matt.

She'd turned her twin down, but she did get her act together. If Matt didn't think enough of their relationship to try to contact her, to try to make her understand why he'd changed so radically from lover to stranger, then to hell with him. He was dead to her, she resolved. And he'd remained that way.

Until twenty minutes ago.

The adrenaline in her veins kept mounting.

Natalie focused on her driving. Vegas in the daylight wasn't nearly as alluring, as magical and glitzy as it was after dark. Like an aging woman best seen in soft lighting, Vegas's imperfections were all visible in the daylight. Natalie supposed that was why people like her sister didn't like to get up until noon. They lived for the night.

Except that Candace could no longer do that.

The thought brought a fresh, sharp ache with it.

"Damn it, Candy, what a waste," Natalie murmured under her breath.

She pulled up before the Janus casino. One of the three valets currently on duty came to life and made a beeline for her vehicle.

"Welcome to the Janus," the young attendant said cheerfully as he opened her door with a flourish.

"We'll see," she replied solemnly.

As he pulled away with her car, Natalie looked up at the casino's logo. Janus was the Roman god with two faces, one pointed toward the past, the other facing the future. It struck her as rather ironic, given what she was doing here, seeking out someone from her past in order to get answers so that the future could be settled.

The moment she entered the casino, the Vegas phenomena took hold. It was like stepping into a world where time did not matter or even make an appearance. There was only a sense of "now."

Because in Natalie's experience she'd discovered that bartenders knew the inner workings of any establishment they worked for better than anyone else, she made her way to the first bar she saw within the casino.

The bartender in attendance was a gregarious man in his early forties. He had a quick, sexy smile, which was probably one of the main reasons he'd been hired. His name tag identified him as Kevin.

Moving to her end of the bar, Kevin asked, "What'll it be, pretty lady?"

"Information." She saw a dubious look cross his brow. To counter that, she took out her badge. Granted she wasn't here in an official capacity, but Kevin didn't need to know that. "Were you on duty last night?"

Kevin began to wipe the gleaming black surface of the bar. "You mean during the gala?"

"Yes."

The smile gracing his lips was a satisfied one. Last night had obviously been profitable for him, she judged. "I caught an extra shift."

She took out Candace's photograph and carefully placed it on the bar. "Did you happen to see this woman there?"

The bartender glanced at the picture. Mild interest turned to recognition. "You mean Candace Rothchild? Yeah, she was here, loud and brassy as always. But not for long," he added, looking rather disappointed. There was always a circus when Candace was around, Natalie thought. "She and the boss had at it and then he had our head of security escort her out."

She latched onto the first part of his statement. "They argued? About what?"

He shook his head. "Couldn't tell you. Too far away for anything but body language," he confessed.

"And the head of security?" she asked.

"He got her to leave."

She leaned in over the bar. "Tell me about him."

"Don't know much," the bartender admitted. "Just that his name's Matt Shaffer. Boss flew him in from L.A., where he was head of security for Montgomery Enterprises."

There was no avoiding it, she thought darkly. She was going to have to talk to Matt. The thought left her cold. "Do you know where I can find him right now?"

Kevin glanced at his watch. "He should be in his office. On the second floor, toward the rear." He gave her the numbers of the rooms where the monitors that kept watch over the casino guests as they tried their luck against the house were located.

Taking out a twenty, she placed it on the bar. "Thanks for your help."

Kevin slipped the bill into his vest pocket. "Any time, lovely lady," he called after her. "Any time."

She debated going up the stairs, then decided on the elevator. The car that took her up to the second floor was empty. Natalie stepped out of the elevator, looked around to get her bearings and then walked toward the rear of the floor.

"Into the Valley of Death rode the six hundred," she silently recited, digging deep for a line from a poem by Tennyson. Wrapping her hand around a brass handle, she opened one of the glass doors and walked in.

The woman whose desk was closest to the door looked up. "You can't come in here. This is a restricted area."

Natalie already had her ID in her hand and held it up. "I'm looking for Matt Shaffer," she told the woman.

God, even saying his name made her mouth go dry. She was supposed to be over him, to have moved on with her life. What happened?

The woman began to answer her. "He's—"

"Right here."

The deep voice came from behind her. Natalie felt every single nerve ending go on tactical alert at the same moment that all the hairs at the back of her neck stood up. Eight years had passed, but she would have recognized his voice anywhere.

* * * * *

*Why did Matt Shaffer leave
heiress-turned-cop Natalie Rothchild?
What does he know about the death of
Natalie's twin sister?
Come and meet these two reunited lovers
and learn the secrets of the Rothchild family in
THE HEIRESS'S 2-WEEK AFFAIR
by USA TODAY bestselling author
Marie Ferrarella.
The first book in Silhouette® Romantic Suspense's
wildly romantic new continuity,
LOVE IN 60 SECONDS!
Available April 2009.*

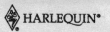

Undone!

THE RAKE'S INHERITED COURTESAN
Ann Lethbridge

Christopher Evernden has been
assigned the unfortunate task of minding
Parisian courtesan Sylvia Boisette.
When Syliva sets off to find her father,
Christopher has no choice but to follow
and finds her kidnapped by an Irishman.
Once rescued, they finally succumb to
the temptation that has been brewing
between them. But can they see past the
limitations such a love can bring?

Available April 2009
wherever books are sold.

The Inside Romance newsletter has a NEW look for the new year!

Same great content, brand-new look!

The Inside Romance newsletter is a FREE quarterly newsletter highlighting our upcoming series releases and promotions!

Click on the Inside Romance link on the front page of **www.eHarlequin.com** or e-mail us at insideromance@harlequin.ca to sign up to receive your FREE newsletter today!

You can also subscribe by writing to us at: HARLEQUIN BOOKS Attention: Customer Service Department P.O. Box 9057, Buffalo, NY 14269-9057

Please allow 4-6 weeks for delivery of the first issue by mail.

IRNNEW09

REQUEST YOUR FREE BOOKS!
2 FREE NOVELS PLUS 2
FREE GIFTS!

HARLEQUIN ROMANCE

From the Heart, For the Heart

YES! Please send me 2 FREE Harlequin Romance® novels and my 2 FREE gifts (gifts are worth about $10). After receiving them, if I don't wish to receive any more books, I can return the shipping statement marked "cancel." If I don't cancel, I will receive 4 brand-new novels every month and be billed just $3.32 per book in the U.S. or $3.80 per book in Canada, plus 25¢ shipping and handling per book and applicable taxes, if any*. That's a savings of over 15% off the cover price! I understand that accepting the 2 free books and gifts places me under no obligation to buy anything. I can always return a shipment and cancel at any time. Even if I never buy another book, the two free books and gifts are mine to keep forever.

114 HDN ERQW   314 HDN ERQ9

Name _____ (PLEASE PRINT) _____

Address _____ Apt. # _____

City _____ State/Prov. _____ Zip/Postal Code _____

Signature (if under 18, a parent or guardian must sign)

Mail to the **Harlequin Reader Service:**
IN U.S.A.: P.O. Box 1867, Buffalo, NY 14240-1867
IN CANADA: P.O. Box 609, Fort Erie, Ontario L2A 5X3

Not valid to current subscribers of Harlequin Romance books.

Want to try two free books from another line?
Call 1-800-873-8635 or visit www.morefreebooks.com.

* Terms and prices subject to change without notice. N.Y. residents add applicable sales tax. Canadian residents will be charged applicable provincial taxes and GST. Offer not valid in Quebec. This offer is limited to one order per household. All orders subject to approval. Credit or debit balances in a customer's account(s) may be offset by any other outstanding balance owed by or to the customer. Please allow 4 to 6 weeks for delivery. Offer available while quantities last.

Your Privacy: Harlequin Books is committed to protecting your privacy. Our Privacy Policy is available online at www.eHarlequin.com or upon request from the Reader Service. From time to time we make our lists of customers available to reputable third parties who may have a product or service of interest to you. If you would prefer we not share your name and address, please check here. ☐

HR08R

Coming Next Month

Available April 14, 2009

This month Harlequin Romance® brings you a new story by *New York Times* bestselling author Diana Palmer, and the start of can't-miss trilogy *www.blinddatebrides.com!*

#4087 DIAMOND IN THE ROUGH Diana Palmer

A brand-new story from *The Men of Medicine Ridge*. When Sassy discovers that cowboy John is secretly a millionaire, she thinks he's just been playing with her. John must convince Sassy that he's the man she first thought he was—a diamond in the rough.

#4088 THE COWBOY AND THE PRINCESS Myrna Mackenzie
Western Weddings

When reclusive rancher Owen is asked to look after defiant Princess Delfyne, he can't say no. He *should* say no—Delfyne is regal, gorgeous and betrothed to another man!

#4089 SECRET BABY, SURPRISE PARENTS Liz Fielding
Baby on Board

Grace told herself that surrogacy for her sister was selfless, but she secretly longed for the baby to be her own. Josh wished they were his to take care of. When tragedy struck, would Josh claim them as his family?

#4090 NINE-TO-FIVE BRIDE Jennie Adams

Marissa joined *www.blinddatebrides.com* for a bit of fun! Her sexy new boss Rick was more Mr. Tall, Dark and Dangerous than Mr. Right. Marissa would never date him…would she?

#4091 THE REBEL KING Melissa James

When fireman Charlie finds himself *Suddenly Royal!*, he rebels! But his bad-boy act doesn't fool Princess Jazmine. She knows he is kind, generous and fit to be king!

#4092 MARRYING THE MANHATTAN MILLIONAIRE Jackie Braun
9 to 5

Successful executive Samantha's ex-fiancé and business rival, Michael, is back! And the real merger on the table is more than strictly business….

HRCNMBPA0309